SWITCH

KEVIN McCOLLEY

SWITCH

A MYSTERY

SIMON & SCHUSTER BOOKS FOR YOUNG READERS

SIMON & SCHUSTER BOOKS FOR YOUNG READERS
An imprint of Simon & Schuster Children's Publishing Division
1230 Avenue of the Americas, New York, New York 10020
Copyright © 1997 by Kevin McColley
SIMON & SCHUSTER BOOKS FOR YOUNG READERS is a trademark
of Simon & Schuster.

Book design by Anahid Hamparian
The text for this book is set in 12-point Latin 725.
Manufactured in the United States of America
First Edition

10 9 8 7 6 5 4 3 2 1

Library of Congress Cataloging-in-Publication Data
McColley, Kevin.
Switch : a mystery / by Kevin McColley.
p   cm.
Summary: Seventeen-year-old Ken, an epileptic who lives in the shadow of his older half-brother, meets a drifter who settles into a vacant
lot in his small town, which leads him to discover a world of decep-
tion, crime, and revenge.
[1. Epilepsy—Fiction. 2. Brothers—Fiction.
3. Mystery and detective stories.]   I. Title.
PZ7.M478414195Sw 1997 [Fic]—dc20 96-30917 CIP AC
ISBN 0-689-81122-5

SWITCH

ONE

The first time it happened had been in the Shangri-la Theater. Ken Corbin's half brother, Leo, had taken him to see a science fiction movie. A spaceship had been flying over a lake of fire.

"This is dumb," Leo muttered. "Like anyone could really do that. They'd be cooked."

Ken stared at the screen. "You didn't have to come."

"Yeah, right." Leo smacked on his popcorn like a cow. "Tell that to Mom."

"So leave now."

"Maybe I will." But all he did was settle deeper into his seat.

1

It started to happen then, with the edges of the screen swaying. A sudden terror grabbed Ken's chest like a set of icy jaws, and a blackness surrounded him. The blackness grew thicker and darker and colder; the jaws dragged him down a tunnel of blackness away from the earth like demons. Leo was a thousand miles away.

"What's with you?" Leo asked.

Mr. Iverson was sitting in the row in front of them. He was a thousand miles away too. Ken was balanced on the fence at the edge of the universe, wheeling his arms, trying to keep from falling into whatever lay beyond. His fingers clawed for the tiny theater, now a billion miles away.

The blackness closed around him, the terror twisted his mind. His fingers slipped, and he fell the other way.

"Jesus!" Ken shouted, and that was all he remembered.

Ken was in a silent place, a warm, misty darkness where memories flitted like butter-flies. He wandered forever before he saw the darkness begin to lighten on the horizon. He struggled toward it. When he reached the light his eyes opened and he found himself lying in a theater aisle with a crowd of people standing around him and muttering. The house lights were up, though the film still fluttered weakly on the screen. Something was slithering down his cheek, and when he wiped it away he found white foam on his fingers. The floor stank of mildew and popcorn. The pain in his head screamed.

"Christ, kid." Mr. Iverson leaned over him, his belly full and hanging. "You all right?"

"I don't know." Ken wiped his hand on his shirt. Leo was standing at the crowd's edge, his fingers flitting across his lips like the butterfly memories, his eyes darting from Ken to the crowd to the floor. "I'm tired."

"You know what that is?" Irene Sattle crouched beside him. Her clothing smelled faintly of sweat and perfume. "That's epilepsy."

"You don't know that," Leo said quickly. "He just fell down is all. My brother isn't some freak."

"It's epilepsy. I know it because I've seen it before." Mrs. Sattle ran her hand over Ken's forehead. "You sure you're all right, Kenny?"

Ken wiped the foam from his other cheek. As he studied it on his fingers, he thought of tunnels and spaceships and things that just couldn't happen. Nobody can fly over a lake of fire—nobody. He felt like a fool.

It can't be epilepsy, he thought. I'm only twelve years old.

TWO

Lost Frenchman Creek was named after a trapper who in the mid-1600s had run his canoe into the sandbar jutting into the Mississippi River at its mouth. He'd traded a keg of whiskey to the Santee Sioux for a new canoe, paddled farther downriver, and disappeared forever. The Sioux nickname for him was Thunder Fool.

The first white settlers established the town on the creek's southern bank. As commerce increased, Lost Frenchman grew from a river crossing into clapboard houses and muddy streets and a thousand big dreams, but in southeastern Minnesota a town can only grow so much before it starts to lap at the bluffs and has to run down again, like bathwater. The only thing left of most of those houses was one foundation overgrown with bracken and broken by oak and maple roots. Ken knew where it was. He did a lot of his drawing there.

"Look," he said to Mariah, "a whitetail buck crossed here."

Mariah Ogema studied the two half-moons impressed in the dirt at her feet. Max, Ken's Border collie, snuffled the print. Mariah was half Ojibwa, and as she leaned forward the light through the trees reflected in her long, black hair.

A twirling feeling rose into Ken's throat. He swallowed it down. Feelings like that would screw up his friendship with Mariah, and it was the only one he had. Nobody wants friends who fall into the silent place.

"How do you know it was a buck?" she asked.

"Because it was heavy enough for the hoof to leave a full impression."

"Oh." Mariah stood. Her shirt settled back to outline parts of her Ken knew he shouldn't be staring at. "Should we head up to the clearing?"

He swallowed again. "Sure." Their friendship felt like a house of cards he was trying to protect from a hurricane.

6

They followed a trail leading up the bluff with the oaks and maples around them. A squirrel chattered angrily, and Max darted into the brush. Ken walked in front because otherwise he would have to look at Mariah and that made him think things he didn't want to think. That made the twirling feeling come back.

"You're creaking," she said.

"What?"

"You're making a creaking sound each time you take a step. Is that from the plastic pants?"

Ken's epilepsy medication gave him such bad diarrhea that for a time he had tried wearing plastic pants to control it. He'd made the mistake of telling Mariah about them. She had laughed—just a quick laugh that had been quickly covered with a hand and an apology—but it had still been a laugh that had left his face burning and a big, hard lump in his throat. There are some things you don't even tell friends. "I don't wear those pants anymore."

"What do you do?"

"I put up with it. Can't we talk about something else?" He didn't want to talk about his medication and its effects. He didn't want to talk about his seizures. He didn't want to talk about the auras that signaled them and pulled him to

7

the edge of the universe. Not now or ever. *My brother's not a freak,*" Leo had said after the first one, back in the Shangri-la. Ken had never liked the way he had said that.

"Let's not talk until we get to the clearing," Mariah said. "Let's just listen to the birds."

A quarter of a mile later, the trees opened around the moss-ridden and root-broken foundation. The river flowed below them, wide and brown under a clear blue sky, with a barge moving upriver, chugging quietly. The clean, white finger of the bar at the mouth of Lost Frenchman Creek pointed in the direction of the current. The old Felder house stood back from the bank as if it were afraid of the water.

Mariah sat on a stump near the foundation and watched the river. Max, his hair as black and shiny as hers, growled deep in his chest before bounding away to chase another squirrel. Ken stood beside Mariah, feeling her in his throat, then ambled away with his eyes on the ground. He saw no deer tracks, but near the back of the foundation he found the spread-fingered print of a raccoon, its pads making round impressions at the end of each toe. He swallowed again.

They watched the barge move slowly. The

heat on Ken's face burned; the sun licked the back of his neck. Mariah leaned back and closed her eyes. The afternoon sun flowed over her forehead and down her high cheekbones, her hair moving gently in the breeze. Ken watched the way her shirt pulled across her chest. When he looked up to see her eyes upon him, he turned quickly to the river.

"Let's go back," she said.

He could feel her staring at him. "I didn't mean anything by it."

"Didn't mean anything by what?"

"I didn't mean anything by . . ." He felt like a fool. "It's just that . . . well, you know." He smacked his forehead with the heel of his hand, a nervous reaction he seemed to only have around Mariah. "Sometimes I think my life would be better if I jumped off a bluff into the river."

"It would be shorter, anyway."

"And I wouldn't embarrass you and make you want to go back to Lost Frenchman."

She smiled at him and shook her head. "I want to go back because Sam is expecting me. That's all."

Sam was her boyfriend, a mechanic at Barney's Garage. He was three years older than

Mariah and in his wilder days had spent two years in reform school for car theft. Ken wondered why Mariah was attracted to him. Probably for the same reason she was attracted to Ken. She had a thing for basket cases.

"I'm sorry." Ken smacked himself on the forehead again.

"God, Ken." She laughed and held out her hand. "Help me up."

The touch of her palm lingered after she'd released him. Ken called Max and they followed the trail down to Forest Road, then followed it to the Hasselquist bridge spanning Lost Frenchman Creek. The Hasselquist farm—it had been abandoned when the old man had died—stood on the far side. A weedy drive led to a sun-burned barn with blistered red paint. A faded green trailer home with broken windows huddled in weeds a hundred feet farther west, and in the distance, the old farmhouse leaned tiredly against its windbreak.

Boot prints littered the silt on the creek bank beside the bridge. Ken knew they belonged to Sam—the guy was a fishing nut and had feet the size of Frankenstein's. "Sam had any luck with the trout out here lately?"

Mariah laughed. She laughed so easily, and

it was so easy to listen to. "I guess. I've quit coming out with him. It's not much fun spending every evening slapping mosquitoes."

Ken doubted that was all they did. You don't bring a girl out here with nobody else around and slap mosquitoes. Not a girl like Mariah, anyway.

"He's never been lucky," she said.

It depends, Ken thought, on what you're talking about.

They followed Max down the creek past a field shoulder-high in corn just beginning to yellow, the ears swollen and silky, the smell of them like sweet dust. They turned when the cornfield ended and followed the grass and milkweed lining its edge toward town. The asphalt streets threw up the late summer heat in shimmers. Mariah's house had been built on the end lot beside the cornfield, where Maple Street ended in a nub of dust and gravel.

Max trotted ahead to the Andersen house, his tail wagging, his black lips pulled back in a grin. Lois Andersen blocked his way through her gate like a linebacker preparing for an open field tackle. "Go away, dog! Stay away from my prize hyacinth!"

Lois's husband, George, was sitting in the

yard on an old park bench in the shade of an oak tree. "Come on in here, Max. Wet on the big blue one."

Max sat on his haunches and cocked his head the way he did when he saw humans doing something stupid. When Ken and Mariah reached him, he trotted down the block to the road that led west to Money Creek, then to Rochester.

Across the street stood an abandoned lot where the livery had been—it was cluttered now with old boards, old appliances, and very old scraps of harness and tack. A small, wiry man was clearing a space in the debris. He was wearing a blue hooded sweatshirt with ragged holes in the elbows, a pair of faded jeans gone gray with dirt, and worn workboots, the left one wrapped with duct tape. A stained lavender sleeping bag, bound in twine, had been thrown to the side. He might have been twenty-four or forty—his face was too covered with dirt and beard and hard times for Ken to tell.

"Looks like we have a new resident," Ken said.

"Looks like it." Mariah nodded toward Barney's. "Let's go." The air wrench at the garage whined.

Barney's smelled of cigarettes and motor oil. Max disappeared into the open garage door just as Tracy Rux, with a red bandanna tied over her head, came out of it. Her green denims rasped as she hurried away, and her shapeless men's shirt billowed in the breeze. Ken's eyes followed her. She'd moved to Lost Frenchman from Rochester with her mom when her parents had divorced two years before, and in two years he could not remember ever seeing her hair.

Mariah was smiling at him. "You thinking of asking Tracy out?"

"Me?"

"I can tell by the way you look at her."

"No." Sure, he'd take her to a movie—maybe a science fiction flick with spaceships and lakes of fire. I will dance with you, Tracy, on the fence that separates the universe from forever. He never went out with anybody.

"That's good," Mariah said, "because all you two would do would be to stare at the ground for a couple of hours. It would be such a failure that the president would declare wherever you took her a federal disaster area. Red Cross helicopters would buzz you."

"I'm not like that," Ken protested.

"You're like that with me."

Well, he thought, you're you.

Shiny black oil stains spotted the garage's concrete floor. Fan belts hanging on the wall jostled one another in the breeze. Max raised his head from where he was lying just long enough to lay it back down again.

Jack Bjerk's cherry red Mustang was up on the hoist, and Jack was sitting on the workbench staring at it, his thin legs swinging and his Coors ball cap perched on the back of his head. Sam was beneath the Mustang, dressed in khaki coveralls stained enough to not be khaki anymore. Jack was always having something done to that car—first a big chrome blower, then the paint job, then the mag tires—and Sam was always the one doing it. The month before, he'd installed a horn that tooted the first stanza of the Allman Brothers' "Midnight Rider." Ken heard it every time Jack went by the house.

Jack grinned at Ken. "Hi, Jerky."

"Hi, Jerk."

"Are things as pathetic as they must be for a guy like you?"

"They could be worse. I could be you."

The air wrench howled like an animal in pain. "What's he doing?" Ken asked.

"Making the exhaust system loud."

Mariah stepped over the air hose to stand beside the Mustang. Sam grinned up at the muffler and adjusted the stereo headphones he was wearing. *"Oh baby,"* he sang, *"I'd crawl a country mile for your love."* He howled like an animal in pain too. *"I'd crawl it on my hands and knees, I'd crawl it on my belly. I'd crawl it over broken glass, I'd crawl it through grape jelly."*

"Is that one of his?" Ken asked.

Jack laughed. "You've never heard this song before? Where have you been, Jerky?" Ken just shrugged. He'd been nowhere.

Mariah tapped the Mustang's chassis. Sam looked at her, grinned, and slipped the headphones down around his neck. "Just a second. This song has given me an idea." He took his portable stereo from his pocket, flipped it open, turned over the tape, and pushed the record button. "Along with *'your love tastes to me like a wine, but makes me burp like Budweiser'* I need something more painful in the chorus. Can I work broken glass into it?" He clicked off the stereo and grinned.

Sam was only working as a mechanic until he got his break as a country singer. Ken figured he'd be a mechanic for a long time. "Writing another song, Sam?"

"Yeah. I sent that last one to Nashville, but no one would touch it. They don't want real country music anymore—they want that yuppie stuff. But yuppie isn't country." Sam wiped his sleeve over his forehead, leaving behind a black swath. "Country is George Jones. Country is Hank Williams Jr.!"

"And country is a bunch of wanna-be's starving in Nashville," Mariah said.

"I won't be one of them when I head down there." Sam patted his stereo. "This is a gold mine."

"No, Sam," she said. "It's only a stereo."

He smiled at her as if she had meant it as a joke, then slapped Ken's arm. Ken wondered how he'd get the new black stain out of his shirt. He did the family's laundry. "You want to run up with us to Winona for a flick, Ken?"

Ken shook his head. Three's a crowd. "Leo needs help fixing up his car." Leo had bought an old Buick during his four-year navy enlistment. He never let Ken touch it. He never let Ken touch anything.

Sam took a cigarette out of his pocket and lit it. "You tell old Leo to bring that car to me." His lips made the orange ember at the end of the cigarette bob. "I'll have it purring."

"I'll tell him." Ken was starting to feel like a crowd. "I'd better go."

He hurried outside into the warmth and dazzle of the late summer sun. He could breathe easier out in the air, out away from the stinks of oil and grease, out away from Mariah and Sam standing so close together. It wasn't right, a guy like that with a girl like that. It just wasn't right.

He swallowed Mariah down. By the time Max had caught up to him at the corner of the Money Creek Road and Main, the air wrench had begun to whine.

Ken walked toward the river, toward home. Walter Iverson jogged around the corner, his belly bouncing and his face twisted in pain. Ken remembered that day in the Shangri-la Theater and turned his head as he went by. Max ran on ahead, his tail curled over his back and his tongue hanging, and dropped to his haunches in front of the vacant lot. He cocked his head as the bum dropped a weathered two-by-four and stared.

Ken hurried to take Max's collar. "Don't worry about him. He wouldn't hurt a flea." He paused. "Well, maybe a flea, but not much else."

The bum wiped his hand over his beard. "Fleas have more than two legs. See, dog? These are the only two I got." His voice held just a hint of a southern drawl.

Ken released Max when he saw his tail wag, and Max trotted forward to smell the bum's hand. Ken didn't need to—he could smell him from the sidewalk. Sweat and earth, the smell of someone who spent all his time outside.

"You've been by here before," the bum said. "With a girl, right?"

"Yeah."

The bum nodded at his feet. Beside them a folded paper dragon prowled among folded paper palm trees, and paper monkeys played in a paper band. The duct tape around his boot shone in the sunlight. "You see something you like? I'll let you have it cheap."

"Well . . ."

"If you want something else, I'll make it. You like flowers? I'll make you a flower. I'll tell you what—I'll make you a dog, just like yours."

Ken reached into his pocket. His fingers ran over a five-dollar bill, but he drew his hand out empty. *A fool and his money,* Leo always said. "I'm broke."

"Me too." The bum shrugged. "What the hell."

He crouched and moved the dragon closer to

the monkeys. "You know what they call it? Origami. Here—I'll show you." He spread a square piece of newspaper over his knee, then folded its corners up toward his chest. "This here's a valley fold, because it makes a valley." He turned it ninety degrees and folded it down. "And this here's a mountain fold, because it makes a peak. You got your valley folds and your mountain folds, your inside folds and your outside folds. You got a ton of them." His fingers danced; the paper came alive within them. "And when you put them all together, you end up with something like this." He held up a dog and smiled.

Ken took it and turned it over in his fingers. The breeze made its tail wag. He handed it back. "Not bad."

The bum unfolded the paper. "Every once in a while they bring in a buck. An economical man of leisure has to learn to take every advantage he can."

"An economical man of leisure?"

"You know how janitors like to be called 'maintenance personnel' and garbage men 'sanitary engineers'? 'Economical man of leisure' is what I call me."

"And origami is economical."

"Its only cost is finding the newspaper."

Ken studied the collection. "That dragon isn't made out of newspaper. That's out of a notebook, isn't it?"

"Yeah." The bum smiled at it. "The dragon is something special."

"My name's Ken."

"Rick. Friends call me Ricky." He shoved his hands into his sweatshirt pockets and studied the town. How could he wear a sweatshirt in this heat? "Do you know anywhere in town I can get something cheap to eat?"

"There's the Starlight Café on Main Street."

"I mean something cheap. Are there any orchards around, or cornfields?"

"All the sweet corn is harvested. There aren't any orchards."

Ricky wiped his cheek and scowled, then looked up hopefully. "I got a hook and line. There's a river, right? The Mississippi? How's the fishing?"

"You'd have better luck in Lost Frenchman Creek. Brook trout, mainly. Head north from here until you run out of street. Follow the field line to the . . ."

Ricky held up his hand. "I'm not much on directions. Just point."

Ken did. Leo bustled by across the road—
long stride; spider fingers; his dark, woolly hair
no breeze could tousle. He must have thought
Ken was waving—he lifted his chin and started
to raise his hand. He dropped it again, stared for
a moment, then hurried away.

"Who's that?" Ricky asked.

Ken dropped his arm. "My half brother." He
and Leo never waved to each other. They might
nod if no one was looking, but they never
waved. Ken was Ken and Leo was Leo and they
were more *half* than *brothers*. Like ice cream and
cow manure, they came from the same place,
but it was best not to find them together.

"What's his problem?" Ricky asked.

Where, Ken wondered, do I begin with that?
"He's worried about college. He applied, but he
hasn't heard back on being accepted yet."

"A business major, right?"

Ken nodded.

"I can spot a businessman a thousand miles
away."

"Yeah?"

"They're ulcers waiting to explode. Give me
a life of leisure." He smiled. "Could you point
out that creek to me one more time?"

Ken pointed again. Ricky put the origami in

an empty paint can and wedged the lid down tightly, then hid the can in the woodstove. "I like to keep my stuff out of sight," he explained, "and I need the can because the burners will leak if it rains. You learn stuff like that when you've been doing this for a while." He crossed the road. He had a funny walk—he held his hands with the knuckles forward, and his shoulders bobbed as if their joints were made of rubber. The duct tape around his boot rasped against the asphalt.

Ken watched him. He felt guilty about having five dollars in his pocket. "Hey, Ricky?"

Ricky looked back. "Yeah?"

"Maybe I will buy some origami. How much do you want for the dragon?"

"The dragon's not for sale." He smiled. "I thought you didn't have any money."

"Sorry."

"That's all right. A fool and his money are soon parted. Somebody told me that, somewhere." He waved as he started away. "Stop by some time. If I have any luck, we'll have a fish fry."

Ken watched him amble toward the cornfield. He still felt guilty.

◆ ◆ ◆

The Money Creek Road ended at Highway 61 along the river. The air was thick this close to the water—thick with humidity, thick with the smells of the river. The house that Ken and Leo and their mother shared leaned slightly toward the water; its gray, scaly siding made it look like a monster about to dive in. Ken avoided a stretch of dirt that still held the footprints from a rainstorm three weeks ago and went up the walk to the side door—they'd lost the key to the front door years ago and had never bothered to replace the lock. He kicked the door open—its bottom corner stuck against the frame—and went inside with Max slithering in in front of him.

Ken tried to think of something to do, but all that came to mind was an image of Mariah and Sam on their way to Winona, Mariah scooted across the seat, her hair shining, her shirt pulling the way it did, their bodies touching, their hands going where they would. All Ken could think about were all his classmates doing the same thing—on a Friday night, Lost Frenchman was as dead as a graveyard and as slow as the river. Ken would stay in town because he was poor and a loner. He was poor because at sixteen his mother had married and given birth to Leo on her honeymoon. She'd divorced and married again and Ken had come out of that. She'd divorced again and was too proud for welfare and had to work whatever jobs she could get. He was a loner because he was poor and gawky and couldn't throw a football, because he feared the seizures that tossed him like garbage over the fence into the silent place, and because of the frightful, frightening looks in everyone's eyes that the threat of the seizures brought.

They all knew who he was—he was a grand mal epileptic. He was subject to tonic-clonic seizures—falling down, foaming at the mouth, thrashing-around seizures. He was Kenny the wonder boy. Jesus would have called him a demon.

Ken clicked the television on, flipped through the channels, and adjusted the portable antenna for the least hazy reception. He picked up the living room, throwing Leo's dirty socks into the bathroom clothes basket, then ran the vacuum cleaner over the threadbare carpet— beneath the vacuum's clamor, the Rochester newscaster was mute and looked like an idiot. When Ken finished, he turned everything off and climbed the old stairs to his bedroom with

Max's claws clicking on the wood behind him.

Max lay on Ken's bed with his big eyes staring—even he had that frightful, frightening look. Ken stared out at the road and the twisted oaks lining the river, then lifted his drawing pad from the scarred nightstand his mother had picked up at the Salvation Army. Using Max's haunches as a pillow—there is nothing quite as comfortable as lying on a contented dog—Ken lay on the bed with the pad propped against his knees. Max sighed. Ken began to draw.

The trees came first, the trees growing on the bluffs, and Ken lost himself in them. He was on the trail again with Max running on ahead, and he wandered through a lead-gray and paper-white world, a world like winter. Something screeched. He looked up to see an eagle, and suddenly he was flying above the trees, the town below him, a barge like a stick moving up the river. He flew higher, and the trees blurred into strokes of gray, and the river was a pencil line, and the air smelled clean as the wind caught and ruffled his feathers. The sun reflected off the water far below him, shimmering in his eyes, as if it were dancing in Mariah's hair.

Max sat up. Ken's head fell against the mattress and he was again in his bedroom.

Someone kicked the side door open, and Ken listened to Leo thumping in the living room—it had to be Leo, since Therese, Ken's mother, didn't get off work until seven. The side door slammed, and a metal latch clicked. Ken looked down from his window into the gravel driveway in time to see Leo crawl beneath the hood of his Buick. Ken set his pad to the side and rubbed his eyes.

The page he'd been drawing on was a jumble. There were trees and an eagle and a river, there was sunlight and sky and too many things scribbled out. In the trees was an eye and a smile that belonged to Mariah and he wished that she was there with him now. He tore the sheet out, crumpled it, and threw it into the cardboard box that served as his wastebasket.

Metal clanked against metal, and Leo cursed. Ken looked out the window. Leo was crawling beneath the Buick to retrieve a wrench. Ken stood.

"How about saying hello to Leo, Max? I haven't had enough abuse yet today."

Max stood, stretched, yawned, and hopped off the bed. He waited at the door for Ken to open it.

The heat's thickness was lessening as the evening grew. Leo muttered softly and leaned over the engine. Ken stood beside him, watching silently. Leo glanced at him, then went back to work.

"I got a letter from the university today," he said. "They accepted me." He turned his head and smiled.

There was good and bad in that, and Ken didn't know how to respond. The good was that Therese would be happy and Ken wouldn't have to put up with Leo during the school year, and it put Leo in a good enough mood so Ken wouldn't have to put up with him much even now. The bad was that Ken would be expected to do the same. He didn't want to do the same—all he wanted to do with his life was to get lost in the woods and get lost in his drawing, to find a place where he'd never have to look into any-one's frightful, frightening eyes. "Good job."

"Yeah, right." Leo shook his head. "I make it into college, and all you can say is 'good job.'"

So maybe now he'd have to put up with Leo after all. "Should I bend over and kiss your butt for you?"

Leo set his wrench on the radiator. "Christ, Ken, you've listened to Mom for years. 'I've scrimped on everything,' she says. 'I work two jobs and clean houses, all so you boys can have a better life than mine.' And then you had to go and become an epileptic. All that money she's scrimped on she's had to pour into your doctor bills."

"It's not my fault."

"Fault don't make any difference—it don't change what happened. What happened was that I busted my butt for four years in the navy painting bulkheads and swabbing decks for col-lege money." He poked the wrench at Ken's face. "I made my own way, and all you do is waste your time drawing those silly pictures of some

damn animal taking a dump in the woods. All
you do is pour her money down your throat
with every pill you swallow."

"It's not my fault," Ken said again.

"Other kids get better—hell, most of them
do. What's the matter with you?"

Ken didn't answer. He watched his half
brother work. Max chased an intruding bird out
of the backyard. "Sometimes you're a son of a
bitch, Leo."

Leo stood back and studied the engine.
"Yeah, well maybe I am. But I'm a son of a bitch
who's watched his mother grow old beyond her
years. And I'm a son of a bitch who never used
some damned illness as an excuse to keep from
getting out there and doing it for myself." He
wiped the sweat from his face and squinted into
the sun. "What kind of a son of a bitch are
you?"

Ken dropped his gaze to the hubcap. He
wanted to kick it. He wanted to take a bat to the
entire car—he wanted to shove a few sticks of
dynamite up its tailpipe. He wished Leo had
stayed in the navy. He wished he had never
come home.

"Who was that bum you were talking to
down at the vacant lot?" Leo asked.

"Just some bum. His name is Rick."

"I don't care what his name is. Don't you know better than to talk to strangers?"

"Don't lecture me like I'm four years old."

"Somebody has to. He could have slit your throat right then and there. Then what would Mom do?"

Ken shrugged. "Save money on doctor bills."

"Don't get smart. What did he want? Money, I'll bet."

"He was trying to sell origami."

Leo leaned over the engine. "What's organamy?"

"Origami. It's paper folded up to look like animals and things."

"Junk. And I bet you bought some."

"No." He suddenly felt defiant. "But I could have. I've got five dollars in my pocket to spend as I please."

"Where'd you get five dollars?"

"Mom's been paying me for the work I do around the house."

Leo grunted. "When I was seventeen I was out on the ocean getting shot at. You're seventeen and you're sponging an allowance."

"You never got shot at."

"I could have been. Why don't you get a job?"

"You know why." With his epilepsy, Ken couldn't get a driver's license. There were no jobs in Lost Frenchman. He was stuck.

"I know the excuse you use. Why don't you do odd jobs or something?"

"Buy me a good mower, and I'll mow every lawn in town."

Leo took the air filter off and held it up to the sun. He blew on it. "See, that's what I mean. You always got an excuse for doing nothing. If it isn't your epilepsy, it's because you don't have a mower."

Ken kicked the hubcap. Hard. "I'm going in to fix supper."

Leo glared at him. "What are we having?"

"I don't know yet."

"Try for once to fix something that's worth your allowance, will you?" As Ken backed away, Leo grumbled. "Jesus. Seventeen years old and he still gets an allowance. And he's giving it away to some bum named Ricky. For organamy. Jesus."

Max followed Ken inside. The kitchen cupboards reminded Ken too much of Mother Hubbard—the canned goods were running low, and there was nothing else but one box of dried au gratin potatoes and Max's dog food. He took out the potatoes, the last can of tuna, a can of stewed tomatoes, and the last onion from the bag beneath the sink. He chopped the onion, threw everything into a casserole, and put it in the oven to bake.

The rusty muffler on Therese's old Pontiac roared down the road just as Ken began to fix Max's supper. He looked through the window to see Therese pull to the curb in front of the house. He turned toward the door when she came in. "Hi, Mom. You look beat."

She sighed as she sat at the table. She was only thirty-seven, but her blond hair was already flecked with gray. Her heavy cheeks pulled the rest of her face down. "The Olsons had a party last night, and they left the mess for me. Who has parties on Thursdays? I mean, who has the energy for it?"

"Don't know."

"I've spent the last four hours cleaning up wine bottles." Therese cleaned four houses a week and worked two jobs—a part-time job sweeping out the bank every weekday morning and the graveyard shift at the Get 'n Go, a convenience store on the highway. "And I've still got my shift at the store."

"At eleven?"

"Earlier. Bernette Schmidt has some new boyfriend that either she's chasing or is chasing her. I'm taking over for her at eight. I can use the extra hours." Therese never had a boyfriend to chase, or a boyfriend to chase her. She'd given up on that.

"When are you going to sleep?"

"I slept this morning." Therese checked her watch. "You got supper going? I'll have to eat pretty quick."

"It's baking. Some kind of casserole. We need groceries."

"We have to hold off until Monday's paycheck."

"We don't have that much food."

Therese sighed again, then propped her chin on her hand. Her knuckles were cracked and red. He hated her looking the way she did. "I'll pick up a bag of potatoes tomorrow. Maybe some dried beans. They're cheap."

"I've got five bucks."

"That's your allowance. I'll take care of the groceries."

"Leo's got money."

"Leo's money is for college."

"Yeah, but it's only for a couple of days. . . ."

"Leo's money," she repeated, "is for college.

I don't want to get into the habit of dipping into it."

Ken dug the can opener out of the drawer and opened Max's can of beef and liver. It didn't smell very good, but he knew that by Monday it would smell like the best thing in the world, if all he had to eat until then was potatoes and beans.

She smiled as she watched him work. "We'll laugh about this when we're rich and famous."

Ken smiled too. "When we're living in El Dorado." This was a game they played.

"The city of gold. Isn't that someplace in Washington?"

"I've always heard Arizona."

She stared at his smile. Hers dropped. "Have you been taking your medication?"

He turned away and concentrated on emptying the can into Max's dish. His medication left his gums so swollen that once Jack Bjerk had called him Balloon Man. "Yeah."

"Your mouth isn't swollen as much as it usually is. Tell me the truth, Ken. Have you been taking your medication?"

"I've been taking it." He glanced at her but had to turn away. He hadn't been taking it. "Damn it, Mom, that medication is expensive."

"The expense is nothing."

"No, it's something. It's a pretty big something. And those pills give me the runs so bad that I spend half my life sitting on the can."

"If we could get you off Dilantin, we would. Nothing else so far has worked."

"I haven't had a seizure in six months. Maybe it's time to go off medication entirely."

"That's for Dr. Lewis to decide."

Ken grunted. "Dr. Lewis. He doesn't want me off medication because then he'd lose business. He might not be able to afford his country club membership."

"You know that isn't true." She sighed again. "I'll talk to him. Maybe we can reduce the dosage. But that didn't go so well last time."

A year before, they'd tried to cut back on the Dilantin, and Ken had had a seizure in general biology—he awoke splayed across the floor like one of the frogs in the dissecting pans. But a year is a year and a lot can change. "You promise?"

"Yes, I promise. Have you taken your medication today?"

"Not yet."

"There's no time like the present." She pushed herself to her feet and plodded into the bathroom. Ken smelled smoke, cursed, and hurried to the oven. Some of the potatoes had curled and blackened at the edges.

Therese came back into the kitchen with a pill in her palm. "It smells good in here."

"It smells awful, but it's all we have."

"You take this, and I'll call Leo."

He filled a glass with tap water and waited until he heard Therese yank the side door open. Her voice filtered back as he dumped out the water and put the pill in his pocket.

"What kind of a son of a bitch are you?" Leo had asked. I'm not any kind of a son of a bitch at all.

Ken set dishes and silverware on the table. He was putting down Max's food dish when Leo pushed by him to wash his hands at the sink. Leo scowled at the casserole and shook his head at Max. "That dog eats better than we do."

Ken thought about ice cream and cow manure. "Then I'll open a can for you. Do you want chunky beef or gourmet supreme?"

"Don't get smart."

"Don't either of you get smart." Therese trudged into the kitchen. "I'm too tired to put up with it."

They sat and passed the casserole around. Leo picked at his meal and pushed the tomatoes to the side of his plate. "Guess what, Mom. I got a letter from the University of Minnesota today."

She looked up. "And?"

"And they accepted me." He set his fork down and grinned.

Therese's smile took fifteen years off her face. "Go get it. Maybe we'll hang it on the wall."

Leo rose, pushed his plate away, and strolled into the living room, as if this kind of thing happened every day. Therese rested her hand on Ken's arm. Ken could feel excitement in it like electric sparks.

"He isn't joking, is he?" she whispered. "I've waited too long for this for it to be a joke."

"All I know is what he told me." He paused. "I saw the track of a buck in the woods today."

"That's nice." She beamed. "Oh, Ken, think of it! Leo in college!"

"It was a nice buck." Ken could feel her not listening to him. "Not real big, though." He could feel her not listening to him in the pit of his stomach. Leo had gone off to serve his country; Leo had come home with an honorable discharge and a row of ribbons on his chest. Leo had been accepted to college. Leo did this and

Leo did that, and every this and that put a smile on her face. Why was it that Leo always did the things that made her smile?

Leo came back and flipped the letter toward his mother. "Oh my goodness, Leo," she said as she read it. "You did it."

"You had a doubt?"

"Of course not, but believing and actually holding it in my hands, why, that's two different things." She looked up and laughed. "We have to celebrate!"

Ken hadn't heard her laugh in a long time. "Don't you have to go to work early?"

Therese waved his question away. She pulled Leo toward her and kissed him loudly on the forehead. "Not a single one of Bernette's boyfriends is worth putting in extra hours. And this—this deserves a celebration! My son is going to college!"

She took the last bottle of beer out of the refrigerator and handed it to Leo. She and Ken shared the last Coke. She turned on the radio as loud as it would go and danced with her sons in the living room. Max barked happily and tangled himself in their feet. Ken danced when she made him and stood to the side when he could.

When he got the chance, Ken went into the

bathroom and stared at himself in the mirror. He wished he was looking at somebody else, somebody with the right face and body, somebody with a mind that didn't attack itself. He didn't have an acceptance letter from college. He didn't have anything at all.

He put the Dilantin pill back in its bottle. All he could do was balance on that fence, keeping Therese's money on one side and the silent place on the other. The fence was thin beneath his feet. He could feel himself wavering.

The music died suddenly. He went back into the living room to find Leo on the telephone. Therese was sitting on the sofa, fanning herself and grinning. Leo's smile faded.

"Yeah," he said, "I thought that was you. Wait a minute, will you?" He covered the receiver with his hand. "Could you two step into the kitchen? This is kind of private."

They did. Ken cleaned up the half-eaten meal while Therese sipped the Coke and fanned the sweat on her face and kept grinning. Leo's voice was a low mumble. The receiver clicked against the cradle and he came into the kitchen.

"What was that?" Therese asked.

Leo shrugged. "Sometimes it seems like everything's coming down on you."

"Was it the school?" Ken asked.

"It was nothing. A guy who I thought had a part for the car doesn't."

Therese smiled. "Well, I'm all partied out. Maybe I'll get some sleep before work." She stood. "But this has been fun, hasn't it? We do have some fun, don't we?"

"Sure," Ken said. He went back to the dishes.

Therese went up to her bedroom, the stairs creaking beneath her. Ken worked at the sink while Leo sat at the table. The cars passed on the Money Creek Road, turning north on Highway 61 toward Winona. When Ken saw Sam's pickup, he looked down at his hands in the water.

"What are you going to do, Leo?" he asked.

Leo looked up. "About what?"

"About the part."

"Oh." Leo shrugged. "Find it somewhere else, I guess." He stood. "I'm going out." Ken listened to him yank the door open and close it with a kick. He finished the dishes.

He watched television for a few hours, one laugh-packed half hour sitcom after another, though all the laughs were coming out of the television. At ten, Max rested his jaw on Ken's knee, then collapsed to the floor as if shot.

"Bedtime, Max?" Ken stared at the screen, then out into the darkness. Nothing ever seemed to be going on. "Might as well."

They went upstairs. Ken tried to draw, but it wouldn't come real for him, not like it had that afternoon. When he heard Therese awaken and groan, he shut off his light and climbed beneath the covers.

He lay with his ear pressed into the pillow, listening to his pulse. Her door opened and closed; the faucet in the bathroom came on and turned off again. He saw the shadows her feet cast beneath the crack of his door. The knob turned; the latch clicked. He caught a glimpse of her yellow polyester Get 'n Go smock before he closed his eyes.

"Ken?"

He didn't answer.

"Ken, I know you're awake."

He concentrated on keeping his eyes shut, on keeping his breathing steady and slow. His chest went cold as she stepped toward him, as if she were a monster hungry for all of the heat in the room. She sat on the foot of his bed. "Ken, are you happy?"

There's a question, he thought. What is happy, anyway? He concentrated on his breathing. In, out, one, two. He thought his lungs would burst.

"Well." She sighed. "Good night, Ken."

She rose, stepped into the hall, and closed the door. He kept his breath steady until her Pontiac chugged away.

The next morning Ken was outside with his drawing pad before either Leo was awake or Therese was home from the Get 'n Go. Max trotted through the fog that had crawled up from the river. The streets were empty, the windows were empty, the town held only ghosts. They headed west to the vacant lot. Ricky was sitting on his rolled-up sleeping bag, his legs crossed out in front of him, chewing on a granola bar.

"You must have sold something," Ken said.

"What, this?" Ricky held up the bar. "Yeah, but just a flower. Some woman around here is crazy about flowers."

"Must be Mrs. Andersen."

"Short? Fat? Could scare away a werewolf?"

"That's her."

Ricky nodded. "That creek you pointed out doesn't have a thing in it. I fished for hours and never even had a nibble."

"What color was the sand on the bank?"

"White, I think."

"Then you were too close to the river. Try up by the bridge."

"I didn't see no bridge."

"Just head upstream. You'll have better luck there."

Ricky nodded, then stood and tossed his sleeping bag back next to the stove. "How's that brother of yours?"

Ken shrugged. "All right."

"His hair is awful short. I never trust guys with short hair. Cops have short hair."

"He just got out of the navy."

"I bet he came out with a pocketful of money. Those business types always do."

"Some. He's using it for college. He found out he got accepted yesterday."

"I'll have to get acquainted with him before he leaves. Does he like origami?"

Ken let the question die. Max panted, and Ken scratched him behind his ears. "I thought you didn't like businessmen."

"I didn't say I didn't like them—I just said I wouldn't want to be one. They have their place in this world, just like pond scum does."

They both smiled. Ricky finished his granola bar, then crumpled the wrapping into a ball and stared at it longingly. "I wish I would have known about that bridge yesterday. They make granola bars too small to fill me up."

Ken felt for the five dollars in his pocket. "I got some money. Let's head up to the Starlight."

"Don't mind if I do."

They walked up the Money Creek Road to Main, then turned north between the grocery store and the bank. The early morning sun highlighted the Hasselquist cornfield and the abandoned theater in the distance. They crossed the street to the café.

"Jaywalking." Ricky looked around nervously.

"Nobody ever gets busted for jaywalking."

"I've been. Cops just look for excuses."

They went into the café. Walter Iverson was sitting in the front booth, his belly gumming the edge of his plate and the six doughnuts upon it. Ken wondered why he killed himself jogging, then came in here every morning and swallowed down a half dozen doughnuts. It seemed to defeat the purpose, unless the purpose was to jog so he *could* down half a dozen doughnuts. Walter was fat, but he wasn't any fatter than he ever was.

Irene Sattle was behind the counter, pouring Elmer Kelso's coffee. Max lay by the door, his head on his paws, and sulked. It was as far as Irene ever allowed him into the Starlight. "What'll it be this morning, Ken?" she asked.

"Two doughnuts and two orange juices."

"Coming up."

Ken walked to the back, sat, and laid his pad in the seat. Ricky stood beside him. "Where's the bathroom? I ought to clean up a little so she don't kick me out."

Ken pointed at a door in the back with MEN written on it. "She won't kick you out."

"You never can tell." Ricky hurried away.

Irene brought the doughnuts. Ken listened to the door of one of the apartments above the Starlight open and close. Stairs creaked, and a metal lid screeched. Sam O'Hara walked by the café window, sorting a handful of mail. Ken thought about him and Mariah. He thought about Mariah's hair, about how she had looked sitting on that stump up on the bluff. He swallowed, then stared at his orange juice.

Sheriff Monson stepped into the café. He nodded a greeting all around as he scratched Max's ears. He had an Army Airborne tattoo on the inside of his forearm and wore a cowboy hat as big as he was.

Ricky returned, his hair slicked back on either side of his head, some of the grime wiped from his cheeks. He glanced at the sheriff before sitting down, then glanced over his shoulder at him after he had. The sheriff sipped coffee and stared.

"I don't know, Ken. Maybe I'm not hungry."

"You're hungry, Ricky. All you had to eat was a granola bar."

"I mean, maybe I'm not hungry for a doughnut." He glanced over his shoulder again. Washing seemed only to have refreshed his smell. He stood quickly. "I think I'm hungry for fish. You said there's a bridge?"

"It's at the northwest corner of the cornfield."

"Sounds good. Stop by the lot later." Ricky stood and walked toward the door, then hurried back. He picked up his doughnut. "Maybe I'll take this with me." When he left, he stayed well away from the sheriff.

Ken ate his doughnut—the cherry filling

oozed out over his lip. He watched Sheriff
Monson stand and amble toward him with his
coffee cup in the crook of his finger. "Morning,
Ken. You got a new friend?"

Ken wiped his chin. "He's just some guy
hanging around for a while."

The green ink of the sheriff's tattoo had
faded beneath his deep tan. He glanced at the
window. "He hasn't caused any trouble, has
he?"

"He's just hanging around."

"I didn't think he had. Still, it's my job to
check these things." Sheriff Monson leaned
over the table. "How are the deer around here?"

"I saw a nice buck's tracks just yesterday."

The sheriff's eyes glowed with a hunter's
delight. He pushed his hat back until its brim
rested against his shoulders. "Big?"

"Not so big."

"Seen any others?"

"A few last week."

"Big?"

"Not so big. But the big ones are out there."

"Your reports are the main reason I come to
Lost Frenchman." The sheriff finished his coffee. "There's no sheriffing to do. Nothing ever
happens."

Not since Sam stole that car. Ken kept the thought quiet. "I'll keep you posted."

"Good." The sheriff stood. "You're my eyes and ears." He squeezed Ken's shoulder—he had a grip that could break bones—then walked toward the door. He slapped Walter Iverson's back before he left. Max scooted out of his way.

Ken finished his doughnut and orange juice and again wiped the jelly from his chin. He walked to the door. "See you, Irene."

"Say hello to your mother for me."

Ken followed the street north past the alley emptying onto Maple just south of the Ogemas', past the old and abandoned Shangri-la Theater—it still had a James Bond movie advertised on the marquee. He followed Max as he skirted the west side of the field to the creek, the heavy dew soaking Max's coat and Ken's pant legs, leaving him shivering. The Hasselquist house on the far side of the property stood forlornly. They walked through the barn's shadow and down the drive to the bridge. Ricky wasn't there.

Ken studied the footprints on the bank. He couldn't find the wrinkled print that the duct tape on Ricky's boot would have left behind—he found only Sam's, intermingled with a smaller set that must have belonged to Mariah. He didn't want to think about them together. He followed Max down the Forest Road, then onto the trail leading up the bluff.

Climbing was sweaty work with the humidity so high and the air so still, with the alder and sumac grabbing at him like fingers. He followed Max up to the bathwater house, where the sun was hot and clean, where finches and sparrows argued in the branches. Ken searched for tracks and found only those belonging to the raccoon. He sat on the stump and watched the river move slowly below him. The sun had burned most of the fog off its surface, leaving it gray and silver, almost silent, with the trees around it so still they could have been painted there.

He breathed deeply, catching the green smell all around him, as Max bolted into the trees. He watched a peregrine falcon work the bluff from riverbank to crest, up and down, up and down, soaring on air currents Ken couldn't even feel. Suddenly it folded its wings and in a blur of black and white dived into the brush, coming up not more than a second later with something in its talons. A mouse, maybe. Ken balanced his pad on his knee and took a pencil from his pocket.

He lost himself for half an hour in the flight of the falcon, in the air rushing by its face as it dived, in the feel of talons puncturing flesh, in the wide-eyed terror and pain of its prey. When he came back to the clearing he lifted his chin and let the sun fill his eyes. He listened to Lost Frenchman come alive, the mutter of traffic on the highway, the distant slamming of doors. Max came back to lay at Ken's feet and watch the river.

Ken ran his hand over the heat Max's fur had captured. He thought of Ricky. "What do you say, Max? Want to buy a paper monkey?"

He rose and worked his way down the bluff. He stopped in front of Mariah's house and thought about knocking, but his memories of the bridge were still too strong to allow it. Ricky was crouching in the vacant lot with his back to him, the seat of his pants worn shiny, the elbows of his sweatshirt ragged.

Ken crossed the Money Creek Road. He smelled sun-heated asphalt. "I thought you were going fishing."

Ricky stood. "I was going to, but it's a long walk to the bridge. Besides, I had that dough-nut."

He turned and wound his fishing line

around a sliver of cardboard. Ken saw the same boots with the duct tape around the left toe, the same sweatshirt and the same pants, and the same lavender sleeping bag rolled up and tossed in the corner. But this wasn't Ricky. The face was wrong, the hair was wrong, he was an inch too tall. This man wasn't Ricky.

Ken stepped back. "Who are you?"

The man smiled. "What do you mean?" His voice wasn't the same either—its accent was gone or softened. "You feeling all right?"

"I feel fine. Where's Ricky?"

The man leaned forward and studied Ken's face. His eyes were bluer and his whiskers a shade too brown. "You look kind of dizzy. You aren't dizzy, are you? Light-headed?"

Ken rubbed his forehead. What was going on? "I'm fine."

"Then what's the matter? You look like you've seen a ghost."

Had he? Was he? Ken backed away. "Nothing's the matter."

The man smiled again, then shoved the fishing tackle into his pocket. "Hey, I take it back about the werewolf. He wouldn't run away from Mrs. Andersen—he'd think she was his mother." He laughed. The laugh sounded right.

Ken tried to shake his head clear, but the man who wasn't Ricky stayed the man who wasn't Ricky. "I've got to go."

The man nodded and smiled. He smiled just like Ricky had. Like Ricky had then—or like Ricky did now? Was there a difference? "Sure. Tell your brother when he walks downtown to walk by on the other side of the street. You know how I feel about pond scum."

"Sure." My memory changes, Ken thought, after I've seized up. Had he had a seizure he couldn't remember? Dr. Lewis had said it might happen. But how could he have forgotten something like that? "I've got to go."

"See you later." The man smiled again, then leaned back and lifted his face to the sun.

Ken hurried down the block with Max trotting in front of him. Max didn't seem any different. Max was still Max, wasn't he?

Ken felt suddenly dizzy. Why wasn't Ricky still Ricky?

"Different?" Leo was leaning over the engine of his Buick, working a bolt with a wrench. "What's that supposed to mean?"

"It means different," Ken said. "Not the same guy."

"Yeah, right." Leo grimaced as he tried to loosen the bolt. It wouldn't budge. "Bums come and they go. One moves in and one moves out. It happens all the time."

"But this guy was dressed the same."

"They all dress the same. In rags."

"This guy was wearing the same clothes. He even had the same boots, with duct tape wrapped around one sole."

"So maybe he was the same guy."

"He was different."

Leo backed away, wiped his brow, and studied the bolt. "You didn't seize up, did you? You know what that does to the way you see things."

"I remember when I seize up."

Leo worked the bolt again. "You scream and fall down and flail around, then you sleep for a half hour. You don't remember nothing else."

"But I know when it happens."

"I know a few things too." Leo wiped his hands on his pants and got a fresh grip on the wrench. "I know you haven't been taking your medication."

Ken leaned on the fender and watched him work. "How do you know that?"

"I keep track of how fast you're sucking Mom's money down. The level in your medication bottle hasn't changed."

Hell, Ken thought. "Don't worry about my medication. I'll worry about my medication."

"Then don't come to me with these crazy stories about people changing." He gave up on the bolt and crawled beneath the chassis to get at the oil pan. Ken watched him from beneath the hood, staring down through a tangle of pipes and belts and hoses.

"Just come look at him with me."

"Watch what you're doing up there. You're knocking dust into my eyes." Leo squinted. "I've got better things to do. This car has to be ready by Wednesday."

"For what?"

"The school wants me to come up and look around."

"It'll be ready without that part?"

"I got that part." Leo crawled out. Black oil hissed as it drained into a pan. "I found it somewhere else."

"Come with me and see him, Leo. It won't take any longer than it will take for the oil to drain."

Leo sighed. "I'm not going to leave getting this car ready to chase after something just because you haven't been taking your medication. I still got to get this bolt loose." He tried it again and failed. "Do we have any solvent? I wonder if I ought to walk to the hardware store."

"I'll go with you. We can check out the vacant lot on the way."

"Forget it, Ken." He wiped his hands on a dirty rag and headed around the house. "You don't have any problem that wouldn't clear up with a dose of Dilantin."

Ken watched him disappear around the corner, then listened for his boot against the door. "You didn't see him. You don't know." He stared at the engine, at the bolt that wouldn't break loose. "But do I?"

He looked at the sun and tried to force its rays to clear his mind. Leo came around the corner with a yellow can in his hand. He squirted something on the bolt and stood back to stare at it. Ken walked toward the road. Max followed him.

"Where you going?" Leo called.

"Over to Mariah's." She'd believe him. She was a friend, not a half brother.

Ken crossed the road to stay away from the vacant lot. Ricky, but it couldn't be Ricky, smiled and waved. Ken hurried north on Maple through the thick, sweet smell of Lois Andersen's hyacinths to the Ogema house. Mariah answered when he knocked, her hair a mess and her eyes still heavy with sleep. Jason, her younger brother, was sitting on the sofa behind her, watching cartoons, his long hair tied back in a ponytail.

"Sorry." Ken hit his forehead with the heel of his hand. "I woke you up."

"Don't apologize." Something fluttered in

his chest when she smiled. "I was eating breakfast."

"Sorry I interrupted your breakfast." God, he thought, why do I always say such stupid things when I'm around Mariah? Why do I always feel like a fool?

His chest fluttered again as she watched him. "What's up?" she asked.

He glanced at her brother, who had turned to stare at them. Ken didn't need both Jason and Leo thinking he was a nut. "Let's talk out here."

She stepped outside and closed the door behind her. The sun shone on her hair and burned some of the sleep from her eyes. "What's going on?"

"Remember that bum we saw down at the vacant lot yesterday? He's not the same bum now. He's dressed the same and he acts the same and he even remembers what we talked about this morning, but he's not the same guy."

She stared down the block. Ricky who wasn't Ricky was a tiny blur moving back and forth across the lot. "He looks the same to me."

"Of course he does, from this distance. Let's get closer."

"Let me get my shoes on."

He waited for her outside the door. The smell

of toast and peanut butter joined the cartoon music flowing out of the open window—violins and bassoons running up and down scales like maniacs. When she came out again, Ken led her toward the Money Creek Road.

"I wish you would have come with us to the movie last night, Ken. It was a good one."

She was always wishing he had done something. "How was the fishing?"

"I told you I don't go out there with him anymore."

He shrugged. "Somebody was out there with him."

Max crossed the road into the lot, his tail wagging. Ricky who wasn't Ricky leaned over to pat his head. Ken stopped Mariah at the other side of the road.

"See?" he whispered. "He's different."

She studied him, then shrugged. "He looks the same to me. Same clothes, same beard."

"You only saw him from a distance. Study him closely."

She did. He was scratching Max's ears. Mariah shrugged. "He looks the same."

Ken felt his color rise, felt his pulse beat at his temples. She was supposed to believe him. That's what friends are for. "Mariah, he's not the same."

"Ken," she said quietly, "be careful. You know what happens when you get excited."

"Yeah, I know what happens—I seize up. But this is wrong. For all we know the real guy is lying dead in a ditch somewhere."

She shrugged. "This is the real guy, Ken."

"Damn it, Mariah!" Why would no one believe him?

She rested her hand on his arm. "Just relax. We'll talk to him, all right?"

"I don't need to talk to him to know what I know."

She studied Ken quietly, as if *he* were the one who had changed. "Are you sure about this? Nothing happened yesterday, did it?"

Now she was playing the poor, helpless, epileptic Ken angle. She was just like Leo, and Ken didn't want her to be just like Leo. "No, I didn't seize up. This isn't the same guy."

"Maybe you did, Ken," she said, "because he is."

A curse rose in Ken's throat, hot and bitter. Mariah stepped off the curb and started across the road. He followed her with blood pounding in his ears, with the edges of his vision bright and wavering. When he reached the curb she was standing on the sidewalk with her hands in the back pockets of her jeans. She asked the bum something; Ken could see her lips moving, but he couldn't hear what she said. He could have been watching her through a telescope from a thousand miles away.

Max slunk over to Ken with a whimper and pressed his flank against Ken's leg.

"Max?" Ken asked, then a terror gripped and shook him. His chest locked and the buildings began to sway. "Jesus!"

He was slipping away from the bum and Mariah; his terror was dragging him down the long tunnel toward the fence at the edge of the universe. They looked so different from way out there. The bum looked just like Ricky.

Get down, he thought, get down. Get down and breathe.

He dropped to the curb and sat with his head in his hands, his legs crossed, his eyes shut, balancing on the fence. His terror was like a madman, dancing and laughing and spitting in his face, but Ken was still enough in control to know he had to face it down and that he had to breathe. Breathe. One, two, in, out, breathe. He listened to the madman bellow.

His pulse was still pounding, but he'd slowed it now. Two, one, out, in, breathe. He could hear again, muffled sounds, voices that echoed as if his mind were a cave. Breathe, he thought, he pleaded. Breathe.

The pounding in his ears, the terror gripping him, eased. The voices became clearer. When he opened his eyes he found Max's head in his lap, staring up at him as if he were about to cry.

"Are you all right?" he heard Mariah say.

He looked up. The buildings were solid again. Mariah was so close he could smell her hair. The bum was the bum and less like Ricky. Less like Ricky, or more like Ricky? What was the truth and what wasn't? Had he really seized up that morning?

"Are you all right?" Mariah asked again.

"Yeah." He rubbed his eyes. His head felt as if someone had buried an ax in it. "I'm fine."

"You had me going," the bum said. "I was about ready to flip out myself."

Ken lay back on the ground, seeking something steady. Max lay beside him, his chin on Ken's chest. The bum's familiar, unfamiliar face framed itself in an intense blue sky—dark beard, dirty cheeks, long hair hanging down.

"Who are you?" Ken asked.

The bum glanced at Mariah nervously. "I don't think he's all right yet."

"Are you Ricky?" Ken asked.

"You know I'm Ricky," the bum said. "You bought me a doughnut. We made fun of your brother."

"Yeah, I think I remember now." But did he?

Ken sat, then stood. The world swayed again, but this time it swayed because of his headache, swayed because of his pain. "I'm sorry." He hated this.

"Don't be sorry." Ricky gripped Ken's shoulder. "Something happens like that, and there's nothing you can do."

Ken nodded. "I've got to get home." I've got to get away. I've got to think things through. Frightful, frightening eyes were all around him.

Mariah took his arm. "Do you want me to walk you there?"

He shrugged her off. I'm not an invalid. I'm just an epileptic. "I'll be fine. See you two later."

"See you," Ricky said. "Take care of that seizure stuff."

Ken was so tired as he walked home that he stumbled. Every time he did, Max was there to lean on, a warm anchor against his leg. The day was different than it had been before, the sun brighter, the shadows it cast more sharply defined. The humidity swirled around him like a dream. Everything was jumbled now. Ricky now was Ricky then and Ricky then was Ricky now; their faces had blended into one or they had never been different. Ken couldn't remember. He wasn't sure he could remember anything anymore.

"So how's Mariah?" Leo asked when Ken plodded into the kitchen. Leo was washing the grease off his hands in the sink.

The world was still fuzzy. Everything seemed tilted half a degree. "Fine."

"I can't understand what she sees in that caveman of a boyfriend she's got. Country music singer? Yeah, right. A car thief is what he is." He dried his hands and tapped his chest. "What she needs is an upstanding young college boy."

"Sure."

Leo studied him. "You're acting pretty scatterbrained. Did the incredible changing man at the corner turn into Abraham Lincoln?"

Ken didn't answer. "I'm going to lie down for a while."

"That's what happens when you get up at those god-awful early hours." Leo hung the towel on the refrigerator handle. "Don't forget about cleaning the house. Mom won't like it if she wakes up and finds it like this."

Ken's eyes wandered the room. Grease on the sink, motor oil staining the towel, and dusty footprints from Leo's boots running in trails across the floor. He was too tired to protest. He followed the stairs to his bedroom and lay on Max's haunches, falling into the soothing heat of the dog's body. He stared at the ceiling and tried to make sense of the world.

"Impossible," he said.

He awoke with his headache only background pain and the sun angling through the window. By the shadows he guessed it to be four o'clock. His head was on the mattress—Max was lying by the door, watching him. The silence in the house told Ken that Therese was still asleep. She'd awaken soon and stay awake only long enough to fall asleep again for the night. She didn't work on weekends. Sometimes she didn't even leave her bedroom.

The side door slammed. Through the window, Ken watched Leo trot toward Main Street. He stood and went downstairs.

The mess still cluttered the kitchen. He ran the stained towel up to Leo's room and worked it into his dirty pile of clothes until he'd wrapped it around Leo's best shirt. If the shirt got stained, it would serve him right.

Leo was already playing the college part—a University of Minnesota pennant hung on the wall, and a stack of personalized stationery rested on his desk. The letterhead read LEO SHUMAKER: BUSINESS MAJOR, UNIVERSITY OF MINNESOTA.

Ken shook his head and wrote across the top sheet in Leo's handwriting—*and all around great human being. Yeah, right.* One advantage of being good at drawing was that it made Ken a passable forger. Maybe when Leo found this sheet he would wonder if he had written it himself— he'd wonder if the world had gone as crazy for him as it had for Ken—but for all his faults, Leo didn't have a faulty memory. Ken crumpled the sheet, stopped by his room to toss it into the cardboard box, and went back downstairs.

When he finished the kitchen he wiped down the bathroom, then opened the medicine cabinet and stared at his bottle of Dilantin. He took it out and shook a pill into his hand.

He closed the cabinet and stared at his palm. In that pill were swollen gums. In that pill was diarrhea so bad that he'd once sat on the toilet until he'd gotten a circular bruise on his ass. And in that pill was the money his mother had sweat out of her forehead working steamy nights at the Get 'n Go, the money she'd swept up early each weekday morning at the bank, the money she'd scrubbed out of other people's toilets.

Ken stared at himself in the mirror. He smiled and studied his gums and saw that his smile was no smile at all. If Therese ever found out about what had happened at the lot, then the look on her face and the things she would say would be worse than the swollen gums and the diarrhea and all the places the money had come from.

"You're damned if you do and damned if you don't," he told his reflection. "You're on the fence and you're going to fall one way or the other." But he'd rather put up with it than see his mother have to.

He tucked the pill behind his teeth. "Hello, toilet. Welcome back, Balloon Man." He filled his cupped hands with water, then drank the pill down. He shook his head at his reflection and went into the kitchen.

The sun was setting beyond the window; it was time to fix supper. If Therese was going to eat, then she would already have come down, and Ken felt too queasy to think about eating. He only had to fix something for Leo.

He thought a nice, potato pie might fill him

up—their food budget had forced Ken to learn to do some amazing things with potatoes. He made the crust from flour, pepper, water, and a little baking powder. He had it rolled out and in the pan before he found that the cupboard where he kept the potatoes was bare—Therese had forgotten to buy any.

There was one carrot left. He chopped and dumped it on the crust, but it made a pitifully small pile. The only thing left in the cupboard was Max's dog food.

"Well, Leo, you'll finally get a chance to eat as well as the dog." Ken took out a can of gourmet supreme, opened it, and dumped it over the carrots. Mixed together and with a crust over the top, the pie looked almost appetizing. He popped it into the oven just as Leo kicked open the door.

"Supper?" Leo asked.

"For you. I'll be out in the woods until nightfall. Make sure you take this out in forty minutes."

"What is it?"

"Beef and carrot pie."

"It better be worth five dollars."

"Save me a piece, will you?"

"Sure." Ken knew he wouldn't. He never

did, not that in this case it mattered.

Leo nodded at the door. "Come outside. I want to show you something."

"Wait until I get my drawing pad."

Ken went upstairs, grabbed his pad and pencil, then followed Leo outside. Leo climbed into the Buick with a grin on his face and turned the ignition key. The engine sputtered. When he pressed on the accelerator, it coughed hard once, then chugged painfully.

"Not bad, huh?"

Ken nodded. "It's getting there. I'll see you. Come on, Max."

Ricky wasn't in the lot—as Ken turned up Maple he saw him through a gap in the buildings, coming out of the Starlight. He was wiping his mouth.

"The origami business must be good," Ken told Max. He watched Ricky walk down Main toward the Money Creek Road. He didn't walk like Ken remembered him walking—he carried his hands differently, and his shoulders didn't bob as much. Or did they? Ken rubbed his eyes, then his gums. They were already sore.

He followed the edge of the cornfield to the creek, walked upstream to the bridge, crossed it, and climbed the bluff. Max flushed a squirrel from the side of the trail and bounded into the brush. Ken didn't see him again until he reached the foundation.

Ken sat on the stump and stared across the river. He closed his eyes, his pencil poised above the paper, and let what he heard, what he felt, what he smelled, fill him. He opened his eyes and dived into the world he found himself creating. He was soaring with a pencil peregrine high above the river, the lazy warmth of the evening, the scents it carried, surrounding him. He was looking down, and in the brush he caught and fixed the terrified eye of a rabbit. It froze and he folded his wings and he was upon it when a noise behind him pulled him out of that world and he turned to see Tracy Rux peeking out of the underbrush. She jerked out of sight again.

"Come out," he said. She didn't. "Come out. I saw you."

She poked her head around the side of a maple. She was wearing her bandanna over her hair. "You don't mind that I followed you?"

Did he? No. He shrugged.

She stepped from behind the trunk and shuffled toward him, her eyes cast down, her shadow moving in front of her. She was wearing the same clothes she had worn the day before. The legs of her denims rasped against each other.

"You come up here a lot, huh?" she asked.

"Some. You?"

She smiled and shrugged. She had a nice smile. "This is my first time."

"Sit down."

"Where?"

"There's room on this stump."

She sat beside him. Ken could not remember ever inviting a girl to sit beside him before. Where had this sudden bravery come from? Or was he just being brave in relation to her? Either way, he liked it.

She looked at the pad. "I didn't know you drew. You're pretty good."

"Thanks."

"The eye of that eagle," she said. "It looks like Mariah Ogema's."

He looked at the falcon. Its eye did look like Mariah's. The trees looked like Mariah too, the shape of them. He had drawn her hair into the wind, and her smile shone in the sun. The rabbit, he thought, looked a lot like the face he had seen in his bathroom mirror.

"She's got nice eyes," Tracy said. "Don't you think?"

"Your eyes aren't so bad either." It slipped out before he realized he was going to say it. He didn't even know what color her eyes were.

She looked down at her lap and smiled— Ken sure liked her smile. He felt so much better with her than he ever had with Mariah. He hadn't once hit himself in the forehead.

"I'm an artist too," she said.

"You draw?"

"No." She blushed. "God, it's silly. Forget I even mentioned it."

He smiled too, and nudged her with his elbow. "No, I won't forget it. What do you mean?"

She looked across the river. He could see the words forming on her lips, but she didn't speak them until she looked down at her lap again. "I try to write poetry."

"Really?"

"I try. That's all I do." She looked at him and her eyes were big and he saw that they were as blue as the sky. "Would you like to see one? I got one in my pocket."

He nodded. She took a crumpled sheet of notebook paper out of the breast pocket of her shirt, held it out to him, then drew her hand away without releasing it. "You won't laugh,

72

will you? Promise you won't laugh."

He laughed. Was this how he acted with Mariah? No wonder she thought he was pathetic. "I promise."

"But you just did."

"I was getting it out of my system."

She handed him the paper. He tried to catch her eyes, but she avoided him. The poem was silly and sentimental and so sticky with romance that he didn't know if he'd be able to get the paper off his fingers. He folded it again. "It's nice."

"Really?"

"Really." They smiled at each other.

Tracy stared across the river, and Ken watched the sky. Max came back, licked Tracy's nose, then lay at their feet. They didn't speak for what seemed like lifetimes, and when Max looked at Ken and cocked his head, Ken remembered what Mariah had said the day before about him and Tracy dating. *"The president would declare wherever you took her a federal disaster area. Red Cross helicopters would buzz you."* But what did Mariah know? She really didn't know anything. Ken began to wonder what he had ever seen in her.

"Tell me your deepest secret," Tracy said.

Ken stared at her. Where had that come from? Out of the blue of the sky, out of the blue of her eyes. "Why?"

"Because you've got to really trust somebody to tell them a secret. Secrets are all the power in the world." Her voice grew brittle. "My dad had secrets. You know, about this woman he was seeing."

Ken nodded. "I heard."

"I wouldn't have minded so much if he had just told me—I mean, those kinds of things happen. But what bothers me is that he didn't trust me enough to tell me the truth. My dad . . ." Her face flushed and she bit off her words. She looked at him again. Her voice softened. "I know a thing or two about secrets. Do you trust me enough to tell me yours?"

How could he trust her? He hardly even knew her. But those eyes. How could he not when she had those eyes?

He shrugged. "You know how I've got epilepsy?"

"I've heard."

"I have to take this medicine called Dilantin. It gives me the runs so bad that for a while I had to wear these pants so I wouldn't have to spend all day on the toilet."

"What do you mean, 'these pants'?"

"Plastic pants, like a baby wears. I was sixteen and sitting in class with plastic pants on. And filling them. It was embarrassing."

She was still watching him. He couldn't hold her gaze.

"Do you have them on now?" she asked.

"I don't wear them anymore. I got a little more used to it."

She didn't speak for a long time. "That took guts to tell me, Ken." She stared across the river and nodded a satisfied nod. "That took a lot of guts."

No laughing, Ken thought, no making fun, no snide comments. He wished he knew this girl as well as he did Mariah. He wished he knew her better. He knew he liked her better.

Tracy stared across the river. So did he. A robin sang somewhere in the trees. A squirrel chattered. "What about you?"

"My deepest secret?"

"Yeah."

"I've got two." She pulled her shirt away from her stomach. "These clothes belonged to my dad—they're about all I've got left of him. And the other you already know."

"I do?"

75

"I'm a poet."

The sun had slipped behind the crest of the bluff behind them, and a line of cool shadow crawled up their backs and over their knees. They sat with Max panting his happy pant at their feet. Ken felt as good as he could ever remember feeling.

"I got to go," she said after the shadow had filled the clearing. "My mom."

"Sure." Ken watched her stand. "See you, Tracy."

"See you." She walked across the foundation into the trees.

"Soon, I hope," he called after her. He looked at the poem in his hand, then put it in his pocket. He smiled as he thought about it.

Max looked at him again and cocked his head, and Ken had to laugh. He wondered if this was how a stud felt—one of those guys with sculpted hair, gold chain necklaces, and Playboy bunnies on each arm. He watched the way the shadows moved on the slope across the river. He closed his eyes for a moment, then picked up his pencil.

When he came out of his drawing fifteen minutes later, he saw the bluff and the river with the maples reflected in it laid out across the paper. The sun blushed, and the sky held a smile.

It didn't take him long to see that all the world was Tracy.

Ken drew for another half hour,
and the world on his pad filled with the river
and the wind and falcons and Tracy. When he
stopped to sharpen his pencil he was sitting in a
darkening shadow, but with the sky still bright
above him and the river shining. The birds
argued in the trees around him, and the insects
had begun their evening dance. Max was
pulling burrs from his coat. Ken put his pencil in
his pocket and waited for him to finish.

"Let's head back, buddy."

They walked down the bluff into Lost
Frenchman. Ken hardly noticed when he passed
Mariah's house; he hardly noticed the thick

perfume hanging in the air over the Andersens'. Ricky wasn't in the lot. Leo was sitting in the living room, watching a baseball game on the television.

Leo looked up. "What's with you?"

"What do you mean?"

"You've got a big, dumb grin on your face. What's so funny?"

What was so funny? Ken didn't know. He shrugged. "Who's winning?"

"Twins, five to three. Hey, that pie was something else. You can make that for me anytime."

Was he kidding or not? Ken studied his half brother's face and found nothing. Tracy was right—secrets are powerful things. "Did you save me a piece?"

Leo patted his stomach. "Sorry, little brother. I got carried away."

"Great. Now there's nothing for me to eat."

Leo leaned forward. "I'll run you into Winona for a burger. I guess I owe you that. Besides, I want to show off the Buick."

"Let me use the bathroom first."

Ken went in and sat on the toilet and let the first effects of the Dilantin rush out of him. He passed his tongue over his gums—the soreness had grown so much that they were already swelling to contain it. It should have been a bad day, but it had turned out better than Ken could ever have imagined. There was Tracy, and he hadn't been out for burgers since—he couldn't remember the last time. Can ice cream and cow manure exist in the same place? Ken almost felt guilty about making the dog-food pie.

They went out to the car. Max lay in the yard, gnawing on a new bone he had found—he didn't look like he'd miss them much. The torn upholstery clawed at Ken's pant legs as he climbed into the passenger's seat. Leo got in behind the wheel and started the engine. The whole car shook. Max cocked his head at the noise.

"It's still a little rough," Leo said. "I've got to tune it up."

"Sam O'Hara said you should bring it in to him. He said he'd have it purring like a kitten."

"I wouldn't let Sam O'Hara work on a Tonka toy."

They backed out of the driveway, onto the road, taking the dip where the driveway met it a little too hard. The Buick bottomed out with a hollow boom.

"Needs new shocks." Leo turned onto Highway 61, heading north.

He drove by the abandoned Felder house,

crossed the bridge spanning Lost Frenchman Creek, then followed the highway as it wound between the bluffs and the water. The air was cool in the evening shadow, almost cold as it rushed through the windows. They passed a barge and half a dozen pleasure boats, each tossing tiny scraps of laughter that worked their way up from the decks and through the Buick's rumble. Ken imagined that Frenchman paddling downriver on a cool autumn morning with the sounds of the wind in the trees, with the mist from the water rising. He imagined him running aground at Lost Frenchman Creek, cursing as water flooded up around his legs. He imagined the Sioux watching him and shaking their heads. Thunder Fool. Ken would have liked to have been around to draw that.

They went around a long, slow curve. Someone was standing on the side of the road, his thumb out. Ken recognized the jeans and the worn sweatshirt, the dirty face and ragged beard. "That's Ricky." The lavender sleeping bag, wrapped in twine, lay at his feet.

"The bum?"

"Yeah."

Leo stared. "The hell if it isn't. Let's give him a ride."

"Let's not." Ken was sitting in a car with a half brother who had never acted like a brother but all of a sudden was. Ice cream and cow manure were piled on the same cone, one big scoop of each. The world was confusing enough. "Let's just drive by."

"I can't do that." Leo slowed. "The guy needs a hand."

They pulled to a stop just beyond Ricky, and he trotted up to Leo's window. "Hey, it's you guys. Ken and his brother."

"Leo," Leo said. "Where you heading?"

"Up the road, if that's where you're going. Minneapolis, maybe."

"Hop in the back. We'll take you as far as Winona."

Ricky climbed in behind Leo, pushing his sleeping bag in in front of him. The duct tape on his boot caught and tore on the car frame. He pulled it loose and tossed the wad out the window. "Pretty country around here, but there's a funny smell, like stagnant water."

Leo sniffed, shook his head, and stepped on the accelerator. "I don't smell anything."

"You're probably used to it. It smells like pond scum." Ricky grinned. Ken relaxed enough to grin back.

They rode in silence until they reached Winona's outskirts. "How's the seizure thing, Ken?" Ricky asked.

Ken glanced at him, then at Leo. "Under control."

Ricky leaned forward between them, his long hair falling loose, the salty, musky smell of him filling the seat. "You should have seen him this morning. . . . Did you say the name was Leo?"

"Yeah."

"You should have seen him this morning, Leo. I thought he was going to flip out then and there. If he'd'a had a seizure and died, I don't know what I would have done. You know the cops would have blamed it on me."

"I wouldn't have died." Ken glanced again at Leo, who stared straight ahead, his knuckles white on the wheel. "I might have had a seizure, but I wouldn't have died."

The road widened, the bluffs on the west, then the road, a lake, the city, and the river. They turned east and drove by the state university, the buildings rising high but still tiny compared to the bluffs, into the maze of bars and fast-food restaurants that grow like mold around every campus.

"You want a burger?" Leo asked over his shoulder. "I'm buying."

"Beats granola bars," Ricky said.

They drove up to a McDonald's take-out window. A girl with greasy black hair and a pimple on the side of her nose handed them their burgers and a couple of Cokes and they drove down to the river where they could eat and watch the water. Ken picked at his meal—the burger had too much ketchup to eat in a hurry. Ricky finished his in three swallows, smacking his lips and scattering sesame seeds in his beard. Leo worked his teeth with the end of his soda straw and studied the water.

Ricky crumbled his wrapper into a ball. "Delicious, with a capital *D*. When I come back I'll repay you."

Leo turned in his seat. "You're coming back?"

"He has to," Ken said. "Mrs. Andersen likes his flowers."

Ricky smiled and shrugged. "She likes the way they smell, I guess." Little bits of bun were stuck in his teeth.

Ken smiled too. "Fold me a paper dog."

Ricky glanced at Leo. His smile faded. "I wish I had the time."

"If you fold it as fast as you did that first one, it won't take but a second."

"That first one?" He shrugged and smiled again. "There's nothing here to make a dog out of."

Ken flattened his burger wrapper. "Use this."

"That'll never work."

"It'll hold a crease as well as newspaper. Make me a Border collie with the word *cheeseburger* running down its side."

"Maybe he doesn't want to, Ken," Leo said. "Leave him be."

"It's only a dog, and he's done it before. Come on, Ricky. Something to remember you by."

Ken held the wrapper over the seat. Ricky stared at it. Leo picked at his teeth and watched the river.

Ricky shrugged and took the wrapper. "It's a little greasy." He folded it in half.

"Don't you begin with a valley fold? That's what you began with last time."

"Yeah," Ricky said, "a valley fold. I'm just warming my fingers up." He flattened it out, then folded it again, the edges away from him.

"That's not right," Ken said. "The crease has to be down."

"You telling me how to fold a dog? I know how to fold a dog." He folded the paper a few times more until he had nothing but a fat, white square. He flattened it out again, then wadded it up. "Hell, Ken, I don't have the time and I can't keep my mind on it. I'll be swinging back down this way before winter. I'll fold one for you then." He handed the wad to Ken and climbed out of the car. "See you. Leo, thanks for the burger."

"Anytime."

Ricky wrestled his sleeping bag out of the seat and slung a loop of its twine over his shoulder. He smiled through his beard and loped down to the water's edge, his shoulders loose, but not as loose as they had been when Ken first met him. He studied the current, then looked back, waved, and headed upriver. It didn't take him three minutes to be out of sight.

Ken studied the wadded wrapper in his hand. "He couldn't do it."

"He said he didn't have the time." Leo started the car and put it in reverse.

"But he couldn't. He didn't even know how to begin."

Leo sighed. "So he couldn't, all right? Maybe he never could—maybe you're remembering that funny too."

"I'm not remembering it funny."

"Yeah, right. Just this afternoon you swore he was a different guy. Is he?"

"No." Ken paused. "I'm not sure."

"Let me fill you in. He isn't." Leo's voice held more anger than a failed paper Border collie called for.

Ken stuffed the wrapper into his pocket. "Why are you so mad about a piece of paper?"

"I'm not mad about a piece of paper."

"Then what are you mad about?"

Leo flicked the straw out of the window. "Jesus, Ken, everybody living in Lost Frenchman knowing about your epilepsy isn't enough; you have to tell every stranger who comes to town about it too."

So that's what it was. "I had an aura in front of him. What did you want me to do? Ignore it?"

"If you were taking your medication, you wouldn't be having auras." Leo shifted and headed back toward the highway. "If you're having auras, you're going to be having seizures. Do you have any idea what it's like to have everyone in town come up to you and say, 'That weird brother of yours freaked out this morning'?"

"It's worse having seizures than having a brother who has them."

"Sorry. I didn't mean it that way." They drove by the university. "Start taking some pills, okay?"

"You're the one who said they eat up Mom's money."

"I know what I said. Forget what I said. Start taking some, okay?"

"I took one this afternoon."

"Then take them more often."

"Sure." Ken fell silent. He watched the night come on.

The darkness filled up the river first. Halfway back to Lost Frenchman, Leo had to turn on his lights; a mile from town a loud rumble, then the blare of a car horn playing the first stanza of "Midnight Rider" filled their wake.

Leo grinned as he slowed. "Jack Bjerk wants to check out my car."

Ken grunted. "All he wants to do is show off his."

Jack pulled up alongside Leo, the cherry Mustang and its chrome blower glittering even in the darkness. He leaned over and rolled down his passenger window. He was wearing his Coors cap. "Hey, Leo. I see you finally got her running."

"Like a dream."

"A bad dream."

"Yeah, right."

"Is it enough of a dream to race me into town?"

Leo grinned. "Not yet. Give me time."

"Yeah, about a thousand years." Jack peered past Leo into the shadows where Ken was hidden. "Who's the sweet young thing you got in there with you? You finally latch onto Mariah?"

"No such luck," Leo said. "Just my brother."

Just, Ken thought. How quickly he used the word *just*. The manure was tottering on the top of the cone. "Hi, Jerk."

"It's Bjerk, Jerky. Any demons torment you today?"

"Only since you showed up."

"Funny." Jack turned back to Leo. "No race, huh?"

"I've got more work to do on her."

"Excuses, excuses. The truth is you just don't want to get embarrassed." Jack peered into the shadows again. "You still in there, Jerky?"

"Still here."

"So tell me something, Jerky. Do you buy your underwear from Goodyear or Michelin?"

Ken leaned out of the shadows. "What are you talking about?"

"Rubber pants, Jerky. I'm betting on

Goodyear—it probably takes one of their steel-belted radials to keep you from leaking." He tooted his horn. The Allman Brothers accompanied his laughter.

"It's plastic pants, you damned moron!" Ken shouted, but Jack was already gone in a stink of exhaust and burned tire rubber. His new exhaust system roared.

Leo stepped on the accelerator. The Mustang's taillights were already tiny red flickers. "Christ, Ken, you're telling people you wear plastic pants?"

"No, I'm not telling people. I told Mariah and Tracy Rux, is all. And I didn't tell them I was wearing them now. Plastic pants are a thing of the past."

"Yeah, right—they just became front-page news." He shook his head. "Jesus. How did I ever get stuck with you?"

Lost Frenchman's lights blinked on one by one as the trees thinned and finally cleared. They drove by the Get 'n Go—Bernette Schmidt was leaning on the counter, laughing with some fat guy wearing a T-shirt that didn't reach his belly button. Leo turned onto the Money Creek Road, bottomed out as he entered the driveway, and parked. He got out of the car and walked around the corner of the house without saying anything.

Ken leaned back to watch the stars through the windshield. He wondered if there was anyone in the world he could trust.

SEVEN

The stars were bigger than he
had ever seen them, and they were moving. Ken
was frightened until they turned into big, friend-
ly, innocent eyes that smiled and blinked and
watched him through the windshield. God has a
billion eyes, he thought, and he's watching me
with them all.

He awoke with his cheek against the torn
upholstery and his bowels rumbling with a low,
sickening pain that he feared was about to burst.
He scrambled out of the car. As he hurried around
to the side door, he saw that the stars were just
stars again. He ran into the bathroom, dropped
his pants, and sat. God had no eyes. He never had.

From the stain in his underwear he saw that he hadn't quite made it in time. He leaned back, looked at the ceiling, and closed his eyes. Tears burned along the edges of his lids. I am seventeen, he thought, and I still fill my pants.

He hated this. He hated being a slave to a pill. He hated being a slave to the fear of when he would fall into the silent place again. He hated the looks in everyone's eyes, the looks of sympathy and alienation. He hated how they never understood and never wanted to, how they thought it was just fine to hide their ignorance behind a pitying smile and a gentle pat on his shoulder. He hated the little snickers and the in-the-corner smiles, the little glances that said that, after all, he was only who he was. He was Kenny the wonder boy. He was an epileptic.

When he finished, he went upstairs to change his underwear. The doors were shut to both Leo's and Therese's rooms, with light leaking out from beneath them. Leo was probably preparing for school, and Therese, Ken knew, was reading one of the romance novels she borrowed from the Winona Public Library bookmobile. Max bounded off the bed when he saw him. Ken changed, then held the dog's head close and buried his nose in the fur of his neck.

That sweet, woodsy, animal smell was the only solid thing he knew.

"You're making a creaking sound each time you take a step," Mariah had said. And she had laughed. Jack Bjerk knew a secret.

Max followed him down the stairs and out the side door. Even in the few minutes Ken had been inside the night had turned cooler. He walked across the dirt on the west side of the house and down the road toward the vacant lot. The only lights were the streetlights and stars and the evening news flickering in flashes of silver in the windows. He stopped at the lot and stared at the shadows cast by the trash Ricky had piled in the corner, then he looked up Maple. Max just cocked his head.

An anger filled Ken's chest that took away the night's coolness. He strode up the street to the Ogema house, saw that no lights were on, and pounded on the door anyway. No one answered. He tried again, then again, then peered into the garage window, his hands cupped around his eyes. It was empty.

"Was it you, Mariah?" he asked the darkness.

He sat on the step and waited. Max lay at his feet. After a half hour Max lifted his head and stared at the cornfield, and a few moments later the long grass growing beside it rustled. Ken stood and walked to the street.

The bandanna covering Tracy Rux's head caught the light of the rising moon in shades of gray that made her look ancient. She looked up as she stepped clear of the grass, stopped, then came forward with her eyes down, glancing up only occasionally. Her clothes made her look as soft and shapeless as a ghost.

"Hi," she said.

Jack Bjerk, Ken thought, knows a secret, and secrets are powerful things. His voice grew cold and hard in his throat. "Where were you?"

Her hands in her pockets forced her shoulders into a shrug as she straightened her arms. "You've got me liking the woods." She didn't look so old this close. She looked like a child.

"I want to talk to you about Jack Bjerk."

She looked at the sky, then looked away. The stars were eyes again, and Ken knew she'd always had trouble meeting anyone's gaze. He felt some of the hardness melt. They were really so much alike.

"Let's go sit on the Andersen bench," she said.

They walked down Maple to the Andersen

house—all of its windows were dark. Ken followed Tracy through the gate. She sat on the bench. He sat beside her.

She scooted to the far end and stared at her hands in her lap. "What do you mean," she asked, "about Jack Bjerk?"

Ken watched the flowers catch the moonlight. They didn't smell quite as strong in the darkness. He felt so good sitting beside her. "Did you tell him about the Dilantin? About the plastic pants?"

Darkness hid her eyes. "That was a private conversation, Ken. I wouldn't have talked to anyone about that."

"You didn't even mention it?"

"I never talk to him. Besides, it isn't his business. You trusted me with a secret."

He studied her. She looked so pretty sitting there, wrapped in shadows. His anger fell away. "What color is your hair?"

Her fingers strayed to her bandanna. Even in the shadows he could see her blush. "It's mousy. It's the color of a rat."

"How long is it?"

"A little longer than yours."

He moved toward her. "You ought to take that bandanna off."

She shrunk away as far as she could. He was close enough to see her eyes.

As he watched his hand move toward her temple the only thing he could think was, My god, my god, I'm doing something a stud would do. He watched his fingers touch the bandanna, watched as they slid it back over her scalp, watched her hair pull back with it, then fall loose. Her hair brushed her collar and fell halfway over her forehead and was the color of shadows. He was looking into her eyes and she was looking into his when the sound of trickling water distracted him. He turned toward the gate.

Max was standing there, watching them. He'd lifted his right hind leg and was urinating on the flower bed.

"What color is that flower he's pissing on?" Ken asked.

Tracy sat forward. "I think it's blue."

"Oh, God. That's Mrs. Andersen's prize hyacinth."

Max finished urinating, then wagged his tail at all the attention. They stared at him, then at each other, then suddenly they both laughed. Her eyes were so big in the darkness that Ken wondered if he could jump into them.

I'm going to kiss her, he thought as the laugh-

ter subsided, my god, I'm going to kiss her. Chalk
one up for Kenny the wonder boy.

Lights flashed in his eyes as he moved toward
her, lights so bright he could feel them. He
thought Lois Andersen must be standing behind
the bench with a flashlight in her stubby fingers
and her bulldog face on, probably with George
behind her. They turned out to belong to the
headlights of the Ogema car. As Ken watched it
pass and pull into its driveway, he felt everything
inside him grow hard again. Doors slammed, and
four murky figures walked to the Ogema front
door. Lights came on. Anger flickered.

"What?" Tracy asked. "Did I do something
wrong?"

He tried to shake his head clear and only part-
ly succeeded. "What do you say, Tracy? What do
you say we go out sometime?"

Her fingers played with one another in her lap.
She watched them. "Do you have a license?"

"No."

"Me either. There's nothing to do in Lost
Frenchman."

"We could go out in the woods. We could
watch the river from the bluff."

"But we already do that." She looked up, then
down again. "This is all kind of new. I'm not used

to it." She stood. "I've got to go. My mom . . ." Her voice fell away as she hurried out through the gate. "I'll see you, Ken."

He watched her jog toward the Money Creek Road. Had he done something wrong, or had he done too many things right? "See you, Tracy," he said to the darkness.

When the look in her eyes, the way she moved, the touch of her hair on his fingers quit fluttering inside him, Ken turned his gaze to the Ogema house. The lights were blinking out, one by one, and his anger grew again as each one did. You can't trust anyone.

Max lay at his feet and looked at him with an isn't-it-time-for-bed-yet? expression. The night was almost cold now. Ken glanced at the house again, then shoved his hands in his pockets to warm them. His fingers ran up against the wadded hamburger wrapper.

He took it out and held it up in the moonlight. It should be a Border collie, he thought. But Ricky couldn't fold origami.

But he could. What was the truth?

Ken's eyes wandered to the vacant lot. It had been right there that it had all happened, or had all not happened. But he could remember every detail—mountain folds and valley folds, the way the paper dog's tail had wagged in the breeze. The woodstove was standing in the back corner, an old tire leaning against one side and a shadow against the other.

Ken stared at the lot, then sat up straight. *"The burners will leak if it rains,"* Ricky had said. He'd put the origami into a paint can.

Ken bolted to his feet, then ran out the gate and stood in the middle of the street, his eyes on the woodstove. There was a paint can inside it containing Ricky's origami.

The slap of Ken's shoes as he ran down the street echoed in the silence. Max ran alongside as if this was a game. Ken crossed the Money Creek Road at a sprint and leaped into the shadows, kicking aside the boxes and papers and trash that had created them. He dropped to his knees in front of the stove and opened its oven door. It screeched like a demon. He pulled out the can and carried it to the streetlight.

Inside it he found a paper world, but it was the real world, the real Ricky, and the real truth. He had not been remembering anything funny—there *had* been two Rickys. Ken sat in the dirt, already damp with dew, with the old paper dragon in his hands, his fingers running gently over its creases. Ricky had disappeared.

Why would he have done that? Or why would someone have done it to him?

A chill ran through Ken—something was going on here that he didn't understand. The world at the edge of his vision swirled. He lowered his head and forced himself to breathe—he felt his bowels rumble and was almost thankful for it. They protected him from the silent place.

Max was lying with his head on his paws, watching Ken with shining eyes. Ken scratched Max's ears reassuringly until his tail thumped against the dirt. With the dragon in his hand, Ken hurried down the Money Creek Road toward the river. He kicked open the side door and rushed into the living room. Max headed straight for the stairs.

Therese was sitting on the sofa as if she had melted there. "Hi, son. Where have you been?"

"Out with Tracy Rux."

"Tracy? Is she the girl who wears those weird clothes?"

"Yeah. Is Leo still in?"

"He's sleeping, I think." She turned to the television.

Ken hurried up the stairs and into Leo's room. The lights were off, and he had to shake Leo before he would open his eyes. Leo looked at him with an expression Ken had seen on the face of an ax murderer on one of those true-crime television shows. "There had better be a damn good reason for this."

"There is. That Ricky we picked up today wasn't Ricky."

Leo rubbed his eyes and yawned. "If this is some kind of a joke, I promise you that you'll never see the morning."

"It isn't a joke. There's two Rickys."

"Ken, we've already been through this. If you'd have been taking your medication—"

"I found proof, Leo. I found his origami." He handed Leo the dragon.

Leo sat up and turned it over in his hands. "Where did you find this?"

"In the vacant lot. In a paint can."

Leo handed the dragon back. "Show me where."

Ken waited only long enough for Leo to slip on his pants and shoes before running down the stairs. The moon had slipped to the horizon, making the night thicker, the shadows in the vacant lot more defined. "Right here," Ken panted. He reached into the can and fished out a handful of paper. "Look at this—paper monkeys and paper trees."

Leo took them. "Where did you find this?"

"In that oven. Ricky put it there to protect it from the rain."

Leo stared back into the corner of the lot. A hardness came to the way he held his lips. "So what happened?"

"I don't know."

Leo thought for a long time. "I'll tell you. That first Ricky didn't go to all the trouble of switching with a second Ricky just so he could move on. Somebody did it *for* him. Somebody did it *to* him." He dropped the origami back into the can. It pattered like rain. "He was kidnapped—or worse. So where do we go from here?"

"Sheriff Monson?"

"With a handful of paper and a missing bum who only you and I know is missing? Yeah, right." Leo stared at the shadows in the can. "What did that first Ricky say to you?"

Everything was clearer now, everything made more sense. "He tried to sell me a paper dog. He asked where he could get cheap food. You walked by, and we talked about you."

"What about me?"

Pond scum. "I don't remember. He didn't have money for the Starlight, so I told him to try fishing in the creek. He was heading up to the

Hasselquist bridge the last time I saw him."

"Do you ever see anyone up by that bridge?"

"I see tracks. Sam O'Hara's, mostly. He fishes out there."

"That damned Sam O'Hara—he's always up to something. First there was that car he stole . . ." Leo pursed his lips and thought. "I wonder what goes on out there at that bridge. I wonder what happened to Ricky when he stumbled across it."

Ken watched Leo's eyes study the darkness. He tried to think of the last time they had talked this long without arguing. "But why go to the trouble of switching Ricky?"

Leo shrugged. "A small town, everybody knows everybody, and a bum moves in on a street corner. People notice stuff like that. People notice stuff like a bum suddenly disappearing too. Someone would have been curious enough to ask why."

"So let's go out to the bridge. Let's find out why he disappeared."

Leo took Ken's shoulders. His grip was tight enough to make Ken wince. "You don't want to mess with that."

"We have to do something."

"We can let it drop. Christ, Ricky is probably

floating facedown in the river right now. I'm not going to risk joining him. He was just a bum."

"He wasn't just a bum." Nobody's just a bum. "He was funny. He was an artist."

Leo didn't say anything. Finally, he nodded and released him. "Come on." He jogged back toward the house.

Leo led Ken across the dirt and across the walk and around the house to the Buick. The light in the living room was off—Therese must have gone to bed. "I'm going to drive around and check a few things out. You stay here."

Ken rubbed his shoulders. He could still feel Leo's grip in them. "I'm coming with you."

"You've got to stay here in case something comes up, so I can call. Besides, it might be dangerous."

"I'm coming with you."

Leo took Ken's shoulders again. "You're my half brother. Will you trust me?" He waited until Ken nodded, then climbed into the Buick. It bottomed out when it reached the road.

Ken walked to the curb and watched Leo drive away. When push comes to shove, the real truth comes out.

The whole world had shifted with that one word. Leo had emphasized *brother*.

EIGHT

The sky across the river had red-dened by the time Ken awoke. He threw a jacket over his T-shirt and pulled on a clean pair of jeans. Therese was still sleeping. Leo's bed hadn't been slept in.

Something cold licked through Ken's chest. Something had happened to Ricky out at the Hasselquist Bridge, a kidnapping or worse. And now maybe something had happened to Leo. Ken hurried downstairs to use the bathroom—the diarrhea was bad and he had to sit on the toilet far too long. His gums were swollen, and when he ran his tongue over them they ached. Balloon Man. He took a pill and rushed out the side door.

The air outside was early-morning cool. Ken hurried to Maple, hurried to the cornfield. If Leo was out at the Hasselquist farm, then Ken wanted to be out there too. If Leo was in trouble, then they both were in trouble. Leo was his brother.

The dew was heavy, soaking Ken's legs and catching the light in fiery beads that dripped from Max's coat. A mist crawled up and over the creek bank, leaving it murky. The bridge was a shadow that slowly grew more distinct. Drops fell from its stanchions into the water like music.

Fresh tire tracks ran down the Forest Road, over the bridge, and up the drive to the barn. Ken followed them with Max at his heels, forced the barn door open an inch, and peeked inside. The sun was just high enough to come through the slats on the barn's east side, fingering its way through dusty air to shine upon three rows of cars, all with their hoods up. Ken forced the door open, squeezed through, and waited for Max to follow.

The cars were old—middle and late eighties models, mostly—with sun–bleached paint and missing headlights. Almost all their stereos were gone; some were missing tires; and most of the engines had been scavenged. Carburetors, manifolds, and air filters lay among scattered tools upon a workbench along the wall. In one corner stood a fifty-five-gallon barrel, half filled with license plates.

"Looks like stolen cars, Max." Max just cocked his head.

Being in the heart of an illegal operation gave Ken vertigo, and for a second he thought the roof might cave in. He hurried back to the door, called for Max, and went outside. Not until he pulled the door shut behind him could he breathe again.

He thought about Ricky and what he might have seen. He wondered where he was now. Ken's hand was trembling when he raised it to wipe the sweat from his forehead.

Max trotted to the creek bank and sniffed. Ken followed him. In the silt beside the bridge he found what he expected—Sam's footprints— but Sam's stereo was there too, lying at the edge of the water. Drag marks led up the bank and disappeared into the grass.

Ken picked the stereo up. He turned it on but found it held no cassette. He shoved it in his jacket pocket and followed the drag marks, walking carefully, his head down, his eyes searching. Grass had been bent in a single long track that held an occasional footprint, the heel dug in deep and the toe pointing away from the creek—someone had definitely been dragging something toward the water. Thirty feet up, the grass thinned into a square, bald, dusty patch where old man Hasselquist must have kept a truck. In the dust were the prints of two sets of workboots. One of the pair had a wrinkled strip across its left sole.

"Duct tape," Ken whispered. "Ricky."

There must have been a struggle—dust had been kicked up, and in a couple of places Ken found hand and knee prints. In the grass on the left side of the patch lay a wrench. The blood it was covered with glowed in the morning sun.

"Jesus," Ken whispered. "Oh, Jesus."

Leo had been right. Ricky must have come up here to fish. He must have heard noises in the barn and gone over to investigate. Sam must have been inside. There must have been a fight. And now . . . and now . . .

His legs gave out and he sank to his knees, the dew cold, the sun warm, his breath shuddering, the smell of the corn and an image of Ricky swirling around him. He picked up the wrench and studied it as his pulse in his ears grew to a thumping roar. Max lay beside him, rested his chin on his thigh, and whined.

"It's all right, Max. It's all right." But it wasn't all right. It wasn't all right at all.

Someone was whistling. Ken crouched in the grass, his breath coming hard, his blood in his ears screaming. A voice rose in song like an animal in pain.

"I'd crawl it on my hands and knees, I'd crawl it on my belly. I'd crawl it over broken glass, I'd crawl it through grape jelly."

Oh, Jesus. Sam.

Ken dropped onto his belly in the dampness and pulled Max down beside him, his hand clamped over his muzzle. Through the grass he watched Sam saunter up the creek bank, one hand balancing a fishing pole on his shoulder and the other holding a tackle box. The terror in Ken's chest rose and swallowed him. Max looked at him and whined.

Max, Ken thought, not daring to speak, Max, keep quiet. For the love of God, keep quiet.

Sam stopped beside the bridge and scanned the farm. His eyes passed over where Ken and Max were hiding. Ken imagined himself in the creek, floating facedown in blood-tinted water. Sam dropped his fishing pole and patted his coverall pocket. His eyes scanned the farm again.

"You up there?" he shouted. "You might as well come down."

Ken tried to stand and run, but his legs didn't belong to him anymore. Max pulled his muzzle free and whined again. Ken's breath was coming too hard, his pulse was beating too fast. The edge of his vision swam. Jaws clamped on his chest and dragged him away.

"Jesus!" he shouted. "Oh, Jesus!"

Sam's face was leering at him from the far end of a billion-mile tunnel. Ken wheeled his arms and tried to hang on to who he was. Sam's smile shoved him off of the fence and into the silent place.

He was in the silent place for a lifetime—he grew old and he died there. Things came and went and he had no memory of them. He spent his lifetime wandering through a cold grayness that clawed up his legs and into his chest until finally he saw a light on the border. He stumbled toward it, feeling its heat grow on his face, and when he opened his eyes the sun was glittering in them. Max was standing above him, his long, black muzzle against his lips, licking away the froth. Ken's brain withered with pain. Grass waved around his ears in the breeze.

A shadow moved to block out the sun. "You all right?"

Ken rolled his head to the side to see Sam standing over him. The fear came again, but Ken wasn't going to be dragged anywhere. He was too tired.

"First time I've ever seen you freak out." Sam crouched. "Scared the hell out of me. You all right?"

Ken nodded. He closed his eyelids and watched the sun shine redly through them, as red as a sunset, as red as the blood on the wrench. His fingers crawled quietly through the grass. Where was that wrench? If Sam found him with it . . .

Sam pulled up a grass blade and chewed on its stem. He studied the creek. "What are you doing out here?"

How was he supposed to answer that? Where was that wrench? Did Sam already have it? "I just came out. I was going up into the bluffs."

"You don't have to come way up here in the yard to go up into the bluffs. What are you doing out here?"

"Nothing."

"Hell." Sam rested his forearms on his knees, his thick hands hanging between them. He glanced at the barn, at the trailer home. "What did you see?"

As Ken began to sit he felt the wrench against his back. He saw that wrench raised in one of Sam's thick hands; he saw it coming down. How does it feel to die? He lay where he was.

"What did you see?" Sam repeated.

Ken shook his head. The pain rolled in his skull as if it were a bowling ball. The grass swished against his ears; the wrench prodded. "Nothing."

"The hell."

"Nothing," Ken said again.

Sam grunted. "You come out here on private property, go poking around where you got no business, then lie about it? Didn't your mom ever teach you the difference between right and wrong?"

"You're on private property too."

"The Hasselquist kids asked me to look after the place until it sells. I'm looking after the place. What are you doing?"

"Lying here. All I'm doing is lying here."

"Sure you are." Sam stood and walked toward the creek. He shoved his hands into his coverall pockets and stared down the bank toward the river. Ken sat and slipped the wrench into the back of his jeans, pulling his jacket over it. His head ached and his heart raced. He imagined the blood on the wrench crawling all over his body. Little demons.

"Hell, Ken," Sam said, "I'm sorry I scared you. I sure don't want to give you another seizure. But get out of here, all right?"

Ken stood. His knees were weak; he thought he would fall. "Sure."

Something thumped inside of the trailer home, making him jump. A grin cocked on Sam's face for only a second before fading. "See you, Ken."

"Sure. Come on, Max."

Ken walked toward the creek bank. As he slipped by Sam he broke into a run. With every stride he felt the open face of the wrench dig into his back, felt the stereo jounce in his pocket. Max raced on ahead, bounding through the grass.

I got him, Ken thought as he turned at the edge of the field and headed into town. He slipped the wrench into his jacket pocket. I got him.

Leo was dozing on the living-room sofa when Ken reached the house. Ken went by him into the bathroom—his bowels had been muttering threats all the way home. As he sat he saw by his underwear that he had dirtied himself again.

"Scared shitless," he muttered.

He laughed—never before had filling his pants seemed funny. But he was alive, and fifteen minutes ago he wasn't so sure he would be. Bursting bowels and balloon lips. He laughed again. Everything seemed funny.

When he finished on the toilet, he stripped off his jeans and underwear, wrapped a towel around himself, and went up to his room to change. When he came back down, Leo was sitting up and rubbing his eyes.

"Where have you been?" Leo asked.

Seizing up, Ken thought. Should he tell him? Did he want a lecture? He'd better not tell him. "Out at the Hasselquist farm, looking for you."

"I told you not to go out there."

"You didn't show up all night. I was worried that something had happened."

"Something did happen." Leo leaned forward and yawned into his hands. "I drove around for a while, but nobody could tell me nothing. I went out to the farm. Did you look in the barn when you were out there?"

"Yeah." Ken sat beside him. Leo smelled of sweat and labor and an awfully long night. "There was a bunch of cars."

"There was a bunch of *stolen* cars. And then while I was out there a big Buick pulled up and I had to hide in the hayloft. Guess who was in the car? Guess who came into the barn and started ripping apart an engine? Guess who had some big guy with him asking about picking up a bearing for a late-model Pontiac?"

"Sam."

"That's right—Sam. I couldn't leave until after they did. I thought I was a dead man."

"That big guy's still out there, I think. In the trailer."

Leo passed his hand over his hair. "Oh, Jesus. I hope he didn't see me." He looked up. "Did he see you?"

"I don't know." Ken paused. "Sam did."

Leo was suddenly very awake. "What?"

"Sam came back while I was out there." He *had* to tell him. Leo was his brother. "I got scared. I had a seizure."

"Oh hell, Ken." Leo rested his hand on his brother's shoulder. "You all right?"

"Yeah."

"You sure you're all right?"

No Dilantin lecture; no complaint about advertising his epilepsy to the whole town. Just a good, solid, concerned *"You all right?"* Ken shrugged and smiled. "I'm fine. Did you go down by the creek?"

"I did, but it was dark."

Ken dug the stereo out of his pocket and handed it to his brother. "I found this on the creek bank. Drag marks led from the water up into the grass. There'd been a fight up there, and one of the fighters had been Ricky."

Leo studied the stereo. "How do you know that?"

"Remember how he had tape on his boot? I found marks. And I found this." He set the wrench on the cushion beside him.

Leo picked up the wrench and turned it over in his hands. He sighed and dropped his head. "Hell, Ken, why did you move this stuff? How can we prove it came from the farm?"

Ken sat back. "I had to do something, Leo. Sam was right there. If we go to Sheriff Monson—"

"We can't go to Sheriff Monson. Your fingerprints are all over these." He dropped the wrench as if it had burned his fingers. "And mine are too. We go to him with anything, and all we'll do is tie ourselves into it."

Ken smacked his forehead with the heel of his hand. "Sorry." He felt like a fool.

"Yeah, right. You screw everything up, and all you can say is that you're sorry." Leo shook his head again. He sighed. "What the hell. You did what you thought you should do." He smiled and squeezed Ken's shoulder. "Forget it."

"I screwed it up. I can't forget it."

"Forget it anyway." Leo picked up the wrench and stereo. He hefted them, then stood. "I'll take care of these. Stay here."

He walked outside. Through the window, Ken watched him cross the yard, jog across the highway, and disappear into the gnarled oaks and willows lining the river. A minute later he struggled out of them, brushing off his hands.

"That takes care of that," he said when he came back inside. "Nobody can tie us to anything now." He sat on the couch and sighed. "Promise me something, Ken. Promise me you'll be more careful."

Ken shrugged. He thought he had been. "All right."

Therese's door creaked. They both looked at the stairs as the sound of feet padding to the bathroom came down them. Leo smiled at Ken again. "A hell of a way to begin a Sunday morning, isn't it?"

"A hell of a way," Ken agreed.

TEN

Ken took a nap for most of the morning, then drew. He slipped into the gray-and-white world, but it wasn't a world of falcons and bluffs—it was a world of wrenches and blood and creek bottoms. He drew a page and tore it up, drew a page and tore it up. Ricky in his duct-taped boot kept walking across his mind.

"I hope you're not just wasting paper," Leo called into his bedroom. "That stuff's expensive."

Ken baked a potato for lunch—Therese had remembered to go to the store—then with Max crossed the highway to the river. While Max waded and splashed at shadows, Ken scanned the snags and the far bank for a soaked blue sweatshirt or a toe wrapped in duct tape. He found nothing. On his way back to the house he saw Mariah loitering on the sidewalk. She waved and started toward him. Max ran to greet her before Ken had a chance to call him back.

"What's up?" She smiled, and the sunlight caught in her hair. It twisted everything inside of him. He remembered how she had laughed when he had first told her about wearing plastic pants. Jack Bjerk had laughed the same way.

"You told him, didn't you?"

She stared at him with a puzzled look on her face. "Told who? Told what?"

"Told Jack Bjerk." He felt his upper lip stiffen, pucker, and bow like the beak of a parrot. When it pressed against his sore gums, it only made him angrier. "He laughed. Guess what, Mariah? I'm not laughing." Kenny the wonder boy can only take so much.

Her smile dropped. "Ken, are you all right?"

"You have to ask that? You making fun of me, everyone making fun of me—"

"I'm not making fun of you, Ken."

"You told him, didn't you?"

"Ken—"

"It's an easy question, Mariah. You just have to answer yes or no."

She stared at him for a long moment, then turned to the trees lining the bank. "All right, I told somebody, but it wasn't Jack Bjerk. I told Jason."

"Jason wouldn't tell Jack. Jason hardly knows him."

"Jason wouldn't tell anyone. That's why I thought I could." Her voice was rising. The muscles in her neck pulled tight, as if *she* were the one who had a right to be angry. "I wouldn't have told Jack Bjerk, Ken. That was confidential."

"It was confidential when you told Jason too." He didn't want to be around her anymore. He didn't want to put up with always feeling like a fool. He didn't want to put up with listening to her laugh at him. He'd had enough. "To hell with you, Mariah. I don't need this."

He turned and walked toward the house, feeling her gaze against his back like a shove. He went upstairs and saw her still standing there, her hands on her hips, through his bedroom window. She shook her head and strode down the road.

Max watched him from the bed, his head

cocked. "Don't give me that," Ken almost shouted. "You don't know anything about it." Max dropped his head to his paws. Ken scowled, then marched out of the room and down the stairs, yanking open the side door. Max didn't follow him.

Ken strode to the road and watched Mariah cross Maple and Main and go into Barney's. She came out into the sun a moment later with Sam. What was he doing working on a Sunday?

"Must be falling behind on the job," Ken muttered, "with all the outside work he's doing." He hated them both, but he hated Mariah more because he loved her more too. Love and hate and hate and love. They get all mixed together. Sometimes you just don't know what's going on.

Sam kissed her and waved as she walked down the Money Creek Road. Ken stepped back into the yard until the neighbor's house cut off his view of her and waited. When he stepped back to the road again, Mariah was gone and Sam was turning up Maple with a fishing pole in one hand and a tackle box in the other.

Ken waited, then jogged to the corner. Mariah was out of sight, probably in her house. Sam was crossing the alley beside it; Ken waited until he reached the cornfield before following. He started across the length of the field just as Sam turned upstream.

Sam disappeared behind cornstalks and Ken raced ahead—when Ken reached the end of the field, Sam was setting his tackle box on the bank beside the bridge. Ken crept into the field, keeping four rows of corn between him and the creek.

Sam was fifty yards away, then twenty yards, then fifteen. He was close enough for Ken to hear the whir of his reel and the drops fall from the shivering line into the water. Ken waited five minutes, then ten, the dusty smell of the corn tickling his nose. Sam made no move toward the barn. No big men came out of the trailer.

Sam was just fishing. What was he doing just fishing?

Sam reeled in and cast, reeled in and cast, then sighed and leaned his pole against the bridge. "This is taking a damned long time," he called. His gaze swept across the trailer house, the barn, the cornfield where Ken was hiding. "You up there yet? You might as well come down."

Ken froze. Sam couldn't know he was there,

could he? But he knew, he knew, and Ken's mind filled with the image of a wrench slashing down, of drag marks, of creek bottoms. His breath came fast and his pulse exploded, and he was balancing on the fence between here and forever, but he managed to hop onto solid ground because Sam wasn't looking at him—he was looking at the tall grass where Ken had been hiding that morning, or at the trailer beyond it.

"You coming?" Sam called

The trailer door opened. Tracy Rux stepped out, wearing a floppy pair of dress pants and a man's white shirt that hung to her knees. Her eyes were on the ground. She reached up to pull her bandanna tight against her head.

Sam laughed. "You and this act. You're not fooling me."

Her eyes fluttered up. Her shoulders went back, her chest went out, she seemed to have crawled into a new body. She wasn't anyone Ken had ever seen before. "Don't knock it. It works."

"It works on fools."

She crossed the yard. Sam put his arms around her waist and kissed her hard enough to drive her head back. Her bandanna slipped an inch. "So what took you so long?" she asked when she could.

"Mariah stopped by."

"Dump her. She does nothing but drag you down."

"I know, but I can't." He sighed. "Have you ever seen the look in her eyes when she's about to cry? It'll break your heart."

Tracy stripped off the bandanna and tousled her hair with her fingers. "Have you ever seen the look in my eyes when I'm about to cry? It'll break your heart too."

"You don't have crying in you."

She shrugged, then laughed. Her laughter pounded against Ken's ears. What, he thought, is going on?

"But you don't drag me down, do you?" Sam asked. "Tell me about Nashville."

Tracy reached up to wrap her arms around his neck. "They're going to be waiting for you in that town. You'll be prancing across a stage in tight jeans and cowboy boots, and all the women will love you."

"Damned right." Sam nodded. "I'm a star just waiting to shine." He swung her around, and they laughed. "You sure took your time coming out of the trailer."

"I wanted to be sure. It was kind of close this morning."

"You're just shy, aren't you?" He chuckled. "Poor, shy little Tracy."

"Like I said, it works." She smiled. "I went up into the bluffs yesterday after what's his name—that kid with the epilepsy."

"What did you get out of him?"

She played with Sam's collar. "Did you ever hear about his plastic pants? He shits like a baby because of his pills. Somebody ought to potty train him." She laughed. "I told him I was a poet."

"You're a mean one, Tracy."

"I'm mean for a reason." She turned, and Ken saw her eyes. They were different than they had been—not big and blue and gentle, but big and blue and hard. "Secrets are power. You ought to take them seriously."

Sam ran his hands down her shoulder blades, the small of her back, her buttocks. "I'm taking you seriously." He pointed with his chin at the trailer. "Let's go."

She glanced at it, then shook her head. "There's nothing in there but dirty floorboards. Let's use the house."

Ken's chest burned as he watched them

work their way across the yard. He thought of the night before on the Andersen bench, of the afternoon on the bluff. Plastic pants. Poor, shy little Tracy. Mariah. Everything came tumbling down.

His hand was gripping a cornstalk. His knuckles were white, and the stalk was trembling. Secrets are powerful things.

He crept out of the field and hid by the barn as they went into the house. In a crouch, he ran across the yard to a window on the house's west side, where Sam's and Tracy's giggling was loudest. Glass from a broken basement window crunched beneath his foot.

"You hear something?" Sam asked.

"I didn't hear anything," Tracy answered. "Come here."

The sounds they made left a hard spot in Ken's throat—if he ever got Tracy alone again, he thought he'd strangle her. He shifted his foot, and the glass beneath it ground. His heart jumped. He dropped to the ground to brush the glass away.

"I swear I keep hearing something," Sam said.

"I didn't hear anything. Come back."

"Give me a second."

Ken's heart beat in his ears, his whole body trembled, his throat pulled so tight that the air through it whistled. Something thumped above him. If Sam was looking through the window . . .

Ken pressed himself against the foundation so hard he thought he would shatter what remained of the basement pane. The thumping stopped; the sounds began again. The sun shot a ray through the window on the opposite side of the basement down onto the cement floor. It outlined something shaking.

"Now isn't this better?" Tracy asked.

Ken shifted. There was someone sitting in a chair in the middle of the basement floor, someone with wild hair and something white across his mouth. Fingers clasped and unclasped the chair arms—hands appeared to be tied to them. It was hard to tell in the glare, but it looked as if his feet were tied too. One of the figure's boots glinted in the light, as if something silver were wrapped around it.

"Ricky," Ken whispered.

The noise above him grew, smacking and tussling and kissing, the sounds of bodies shifting. Ken reached through the broken pane, his fingers scrabbling for the latch. The glass shaved his wrist, and a red stain grew there. The latch had been painted over and was clogged with dust; it took Ken a moment to work it free. When he pulled on the window, the hinges creaked.

The noise above him stopped. "There was something there that time," Sam said.

"God, Sam, you're paranoid."

Something thumped. "I'm not paranoid. I know when I hear something and when I don't."

"Where are you going?" Tracy asked.

"Outside for a look."

Ken jerked his hand out of the window. He leaped to his feet as he heard the front door open. His body took over his thinking for him, and without knowing when he had begun he found himself running, the wind in his hair, the grass whipping his legs, the saplings scratching his face in the windbreak. He was through the trees and gone, and he heard no sound behind him.

ELEVEN

Leo was fine-tuning the Buick's engine when Ken reached the house. It almost sounded like a real engine should, though it spit black, greasy-smelling smoke into the air. Leo climbed out of the car and grinned. A dirty smear ran down his cheek. "Hey there, little brother. Sounds pretty good, don't it?"

Ken could do nothing but pant. The smile fell from Leo's face. "What is it?"

Ken's arms rose and fell. "Ricky." He didn't have enough wind to say what he needed to say.

"What about Ricky?"

Ken braced his hands on his knees. He

should have caught his breath by now. "He's out. At the farm."

"He can't be. Sam hit him over the head with a wrench."

"Saw him. In the house." Ken straightened and filled his lungs. Leo's stare almost knocked him against the wall. "In the basement. Tied up."

Leo braced his forearms on the car roof. "Did you let him go?"

"I couldn't." Ken leaned against the house. All he wanted to do was go somewhere and fall asleep and dream that none of this had happened. "Sam was there. Sam and Tracy Rux."

Leo hurried around the car and took his shoulders. "This is important, Ken. Did Sam see you?"

"I don't know."

"Yeah, right. How come you don't know?"

"I mean he heard me. When he came out of the house to check on the noise, I ran. I don't know if he saw me or not."

"Huh." Leo stood silently, then hurried around the Buick, slammed down its hood, and climbed in behind the wheel. "Watch Maple Street," he called through the window. "I'll go around the other side and approach the place from the road."

"You want me to just watch the street?"

"If you see them come out, come back to the house. We'll figure out what to do from there." The engine roared as Leo backed out of the driveway. The Buick bottomed out and he was gone. Ken jogged to the vacant lot. He crouched in the back behind the stove and waited.

The sun dropped—first it was on his forehead, then whenever he glanced toward Main it filled his eyes. Its heat was heavy and thick; it threw shadows down the Money Creek Road like buckets of dirty water. Mr. Iverson jogged by, his face red and sweating, and on Main Street Irene Sattle bustled from the café to the bank. As Ken thought about Tracy and Sam, his chest burned with anger and froze with fear.

He checked the edge of the cornfield beyond Maple and found it empty. Lois Andersen was puttering in her flowers; George was sitting on his bench with his head back, dozing. The Ogema house seemed deserted.

Ken smacked his forehead with the heel of his hand. Oh, god, he thought, I'm so stupid. What have I done to Mariah? And what am I going to do about it now?

Nothing now. You've got other things to think about.

He crawled into the clearing, retrieved the paint can, and hurried back behind the stove. The origami in it was in a tangle. Some of the folds had been straightened, and new folds had been added—the monkey drummer was jabbing his sticks into his own armpits. At the bottom of the pile was the old dragon.

Ken took it out and studied its face. The notebook lines had faded; through the paper he could make out a hint of writing.

I'm so stupid, he thought again. What have I done to Mariah?

Footsteps padded on concrete. The dragon fell from his fingers. Tracy was turning the corner across the road, heading toward Main. She was wearing her bandanna and looked small and shy and incapable of the smile that he had seen on her face not an hour before. Therese's car drove by, and as Ken's eyes followed it back past Maple they caught on the flashing chrome handle of Sam's fishing reel.

Ken retreated into the junk until all he could see was the rusty back of the stove. Sam's footsteps grew louder. Cold claws worked their way down Ken's throat and into his chest. He peeked around the stove's corner in time to see Sam walk into Barney's, the pole over his shoulder, the tackle box swinging. Tracy was nowhere in sight.

Ken picked up the dragon from where it had fallen and dropped it back into the can. He put the can in the stove and hurried back to the house.

Therese was sorting through mail at the kitchen table with Max lying at her feet. Ken sat beside her, where he could watch the road from the window. What was taking Leo so long?

"Junk." Therese tossed an envelope to the side. "Junk and nothing else." She sighed and pushed it all away. "Doesn't anybody write anymore?"

"Not hardly."

"Well, at least junk is better than bills. The telephone bill is a week overdue, and I can't pay it until tomorrow." She rubbed her face. "We won't have to worry about any of this when we're living in El Dorado."

Ken watched the road and replied automatically, "The city of gold."

"That's in Utah somewhere, isn't it?"

"Arizona, Mom."

"I get all those Western states mixed up." She leaned back and closed her eyes. The gray in her hair seemed heavier, and she looked so tired. "The world will look different from the patio of an El Dorado high-rise. There won't be a convenience store for miles."

"And no houses to clean."

She opened her eyes and rested her heavy, damp hand on Ken's shoulder. "One son will be getting his business degree while the other will be a successful artist."

He didn't respond to her smile. The weight of her hand felt like tons. Are dreams just for dreaming?

"Your gums look sore," she said.

"They are."

"I'll set up an appointment with Dr. Lewis."

"All right." He turned away from her eyes and studied the road through the window. Where was Leo?

Therese took a deep breath and pushed herself up from the table. "Happy day, happy day—I found a five-dollar bill this morning buried in my purse. I got something special for dinner." She went to the cupboard and pulled out a can of tuna and a box of instant tuna stuff with a label describing what a glorious eating experience it promised to be. "Well, maybe not that special, but it beats potatoes."

Ken stood. "I'll fix it."

She pulled it away from him. "You will not. If

a mother can't fix a meal for her boys, what kind of a mother is she?"

A car rumbled. Ken glanced out of the window to see the Buick slow and turn into the driveway. He bolted for the door.

"That old car sounds good, doesn't it?" Therese called after him. "Better than mine."

Ken was around the house and in the driveway before the side door had a chance to slam. Leo climbed wearily out of the car, sank against its fender, and rubbed his eyes with both hands. His clothes were dirty; his arms, scratched.

"What happened?" Ken asked.

"Close," Leo said. "That was so damned close."

"They didn't bring him my way," Ken said. "I was waiting in the lot and I saw Tracy and then I saw Sam and—"

"I know they didn't bring him your way. I was out at the farm, hiding in the windbreak." He rubbed his eyes again. "I saw it all."

"Ricky was out there, wasn't he? I told you he was out there."

"Yeah, he was. It was horrible. God, it was horrible."

"What happened?"

Leo stared at him. His jaw trembled. The

sound of the side door banging open came around the house, with Therese following it. She smiled at Leo. "Hi, son. It looks like you've just come from the worn-out end of nowhere."

Leo nodded. He didn't smile. "Feels like it."

Therese tapped the car hood. "It sounds like a champ. Is it ready for your school trip on Wednesday?"

"It will be."

"Dinner's about ready. We're having a tuna salad kind of thing. I thought it would be a tuna hot-dish kind of thing, but it turns out I just have to mix a bunch of stuff together and serve it cold." She shrugged. "It's summer, right? Don't people eat salads in summer?"

They went inside and sat down to a meal that tasted too much like tuna soaked in turpentine—the glorious label mocked them from the counter. Therese chattered about the university and drawing and what a dummy Bernette was—at the store on Friday night she had stacked the Twinkies where the motor oil was supposed to go. Leo picked at his meal and gave one-word answers to all of Therese's questions. He went outside before either Ken or Therese had finished.

"What's the matter with him?" she asked.

"I don't know."

Ken did the dishes, then fed Max. He went outside to find Leo sitting in the Buick, his forehead resting on the steering wheel.

"It was horrible," Leo said when Ken climbed in beside him. "I've never seen anything like it."

"What happened?"

"I parked way down the road, so they wouldn't see my car. I hid in the windbreak. Sam was outside, and Tracy was watching him through the window. He was looking for something."

"Me."

"Probably. He went back in, and then I heard all of these horrible sounds, wails and cries and things, all muffled. I crept across the yard and looked through the basement window, and . . . and . . ." His breath shuddered, and tears shone in his eyes. "It was horrible."

Ken rested his hand on Leo's shoulder. The muscle there felt as limp as the tuna salad had been. "What happened?"

"They had him tied up, and Sam was hitting him. He punched him in the gut, in the face, and Tracy just stood there laughing. Ricky was crying, and then Sam lit a cigarette. He took a puff to get it glowing, then turned Ricky's hand over so the inside of his forearm was up. He burned him."

Leo's nose snuffled, and he had to wipe his eyes. "Ricky started screaming then."

Ken stared out the windshield at the sky going slowly gray. He listened to his brother sob. "You didn't do anything?"

Leo's eyes flashed. "What could I do? Burst in like some damned action adventure hero? Yeah, right—I would have ended up tied in a chair beside Ricky. This isn't the movies, Ken."

"So you didn't do anything?"

"I ran out and hid behind the trailer. When Sam and Tracy left the farm, I came back and let Ricky go."

"Where is he?"

Leo wiped his nose on his hand and his hand on his jeans. "I offered to take him to the hospital, but he was worried Sam would find him. I offered to take him to the sheriff, and he got even more scared. He lit out—God knows where."

Ken nodded. A star was beginning to glow on the horizon; the trees by the river swayed in a breeze. "So now what?"

Leo leaned back against the headrest and sighed. "So now on Wednesday I go to the university. So now you go on with your drawing or whatever it is you're going to do. So now we back off. We drop it."

Ken turned in his seat. A tightness gripped his chest. "Are you saying we just let Sam and Tracy get away with what they did?"

"That's what I'm saying."

"Christ, Leo, we've got to go to the police. We've got to—"

Leo's hand whipped out and slapped Ken's cheek. Ken jerked back and hit his head on the window. Tears filled his eyes; his cheek stung and his head ached and the world turned watery. Leo took his arms in a grip like two vises.

"We drop it, Ken. We let it die."

"But Leo—"

Leo shook him. Tears streamed from his eyes, and a line of snot gleamed on his upper lip. "They were beating him, Ken. They were torturing him with cigarettes. Do you hear what I'm saying? If Ricky was still out there, then it would be different, but he's not. If you go back out there . . ."

Ken struggled, then gave up and collapsed against the door. He couldn't fight the look on Leo's face. He couldn't fight his brother's eyes. "Yeah, I know."

"Then let it go."

"All right. I'll let it go."

Leo released him and wiped his nose. "Don't

lie to me, Ken. Brothers don't lie to brothers. You going to let it go?"

"I'll let it go."

"All right." Leo collapsed into his seat and looked out at the night. "Maybe there will be another time."

"Yeah." Ken collapsed into his seat too. "Maybe."

The star was glowing brighter, the trees swaying more. Someone yanked the side door open, and Max trotted out in front of the car to squat in the lawn. "That damned dog of yours," Leo said. "Always pooping everywhere."

"You'll miss him when you're gone," Ken said.

"Probably. Sorry about slapping you."

Ken wondered if anything ever came out right. Some things, maybe. He looked at his brother.

"Don't worry about it," he said.

Ken spent Tuesday afternoon on the toilet, managing to sneak in doing the laundry and taking a walk with Max in the bluffs when the diarrhea allowed. Other guys his age had their friends and their girlfriends, had their brothers and their sisters and their parents and their cars. Ken's father was gone and his mother was too tired or too busy. He didn't have a girlfriend or a driver's license. Leo had retreated into a private world, taking long drives in the Buick or spending hours in his bedroom getting ready for his college visit—doing his best to keep from thinking about what had happened, Ken suspected. Ken used to have a friend named

Mariah, but he'd made a mess of that.

He did the dishes after dinner while Therese fussed over the clothes Leo was going to wear on his visit to the university the next morning. She had insisted on buying him a new pair of dress pants, a shirt from JCPenney, and a tie. As Leo dressed to model for her, he called Ken in to his room. He handed him a duffel bag and his car keys.

"Go put this out in the trunk," he said. "Don't let Mom see you."

Ken opened the bag when he got outside. It contained a pair of jeans, a T–shirt, and Leo's old basketball shoes. In the trunk he found a tarnished doorknob lying beside the jack. He brought it into the house.

"I picked it up at a garage sale," Leo said when he asked. "Thought I'd fix the front door." He pulled his tie tight.

Ken set the knob on the desk. "You look like a goof wearing that."

"I know what I look like. But what can I do? You know Mom." He sighed as he went down to the living room, where Therese was waiting.

The next morning, black thunderheads rolled over the bluffs to the west. Ken lay in bed with Max breathing softly beside him and listened to the rain whisper on the pane. He could hear Therese fussing over Leo in the kitchen, and Leo complaining about her fussing. Through the window he watched Leo jog out to the Buick, the tie flying back over his shoulder and his dress shoes slipping in the mud. He drove away.

Ken rolled on his back and stared at the ceiling. The telephone receiver clicked against its cradle. He heard Therese telling the bank that she wouldn't be in to sweep today.

"I'm so nervous about this visit that I wouldn't be able to keep my mind on what I'm doing," she'd said the night before. "I'd probably end up waxing the carpeting."

"It's just a visit, Mom," Leo had said. "Nothing rides on it."

"College visits," Therese had said, "are college visits."

The rain was falling harder now, a murmur instead of a whisper. Ken thought about how he would spend the day.

Leo came back a half hour later, mud on his pants, his cheeks, and the elbows of his new shirt. Ken was just sitting down with Therese at the kitchen table for breakfast. Her face blanched. "What happened to you?"

"I slipped putting gas in the car." Leo wiped the rain from his eyes. "It's these damned dress shoes. No traction."

Therese stood and bustled around the table. Her fingers worked feverishly at his tie. "I'll run them down to the laundromat right away. It won't take but forty-five minutes."

"I don't have time." The earthy smell of the mud on Leo's shoes filled the room. The smell of his sweat mixed with it. "I'll have to wear something else."

"You haven't had a new outfit since you went in the navy. That old stuff won't even fit. I won't have my boy looking like poor white trash on his first day of college."

"Mom," Leo complained, "my first day of college isn't until September."

"I'll get the laundry basket." She hurried into the bathroom as Leo shucked off his shoes, his pants, and his shirt. He stood in his underwear as she hurried back. She'd thrown her jacket over her shoulders.

"Don't just stand there," she said as she stuffed his clothes into the basket. "Go wash up." She yanked open the door and jogged out into the rain. Her car muffler roared like the thunder.

Max lay on the floor with his head cocked at

Leo. Leo shook his head at him as if this were his fault. "I should have just gone. I should have just changed into my old clothes and washed my face in a bathroom somewhere and gone."

Ken put his cereal bowl in the sink. "Where'd you go for gas?"

"The Get 'n Go."

"That has an asphalt lot. Where'd you find the mud?"

"There was a line at the pumps, so I parked on the side and went in for a pop. I slipped coming out." Leo pushed by him to rub water over his face. He shook his head at his feet. "Those damned dress shoes—these socks are soaking wet. Would you mind running up and getting me another pair?"

Ken nodded and climbed the stairs. Leo's room was as messy as always—yesterday's clothes were on the floor and the bedsheets were scattered. A dirty pair of underwear hung from the handle of his desk drawer.

"Jesus, Leo," Ken muttered. "The hamper is only three feet away." He picked up the underwear by the cleanest part of the waistband. He imagined little animals storming up his arm. Something in the cracked open drawer glinted, something it took him a moment to recognize.

He dropped the underwear.

He was staring at Sam's stereo. A cassette tape rested beside it.

"I thought you threw this in the river, Leo," Ken said quietly. He took them out and read the cassette label—the front side had scrawled across it CRAWLING A COUNTRY MILE, and on the other side was written MAKES ME BURP LIKE BUDWEISER.

He put the tape in the recorder and pushed the play button, expecting to hear an animal-in-pain song sung by Sam's animal-in-pain voice. He heard nothing but what sounded like chewing, a car driving by, and someone scraping a foot over dirt. He held down the fast-forward button. When the chipmunk chatter of voices came out of the speaker, he released it.

> *"Some woman around here is crazy about flowers,"* he heard Ricky say.
> *"Must be Mrs. Andersen,"* he heard himself answer.
> *"Short? Fat? Could scare away a werewolf?"*
> *"That's the one."*

Ken looked to the door, to as much of the stairs as he could see. He heard Leo pacing.

What, he thought, is this? Why did his brother have a recording of him and Ricky talking? Why was it on Sam's stereo? And why had Leo lied to him about throwing it in the river?

Ken put the cassette and stereo back into the drawer and went downstairs with the questions hammering him. Leo was sitting at the table. Ken handed him the socks.

"Leo?"

"Yeah?"

Ken stared into his brother's face. Why had Leo lied? And if he had lied before, could Ken trust him now? Ken was suddenly very afraid of his brother. "I wish you'd put your dirty clothes in the hamper. I'm getting tired of doing it for you."

Leo laughed as he slid a stocking over his foot. "Listen to you—old mother hen. I just figure you need to earn your allowance."

Therese was back in half an hour, shaking rain from her hair. "I used the big industrial dryer," she explained, "to cut down on the time. Leo, get dressed."

Leo obeyed. He stepped out the door, then stuck his head back in. "I'll be back by seven, full of news."

Therese smiled. "Get out of here, college boy.

Have a good time." She shooed him out the door. Ken watched the Buick disappear down the highway into the gray of falling rain.

Ken spent the day staring at the rain and trying to draw and trying to figure out Leo. At three he watched a television talk show about guys who liked to dress up like their mothers. Halfway through it he'd had enough. He pulled on his raincoat and headed for the door. Max followed him.

"Where you going?" Therese was sipping tea at the kitchen table.

"For a walk," he said. "I feel cooped up."

"I'm going to take a nap. It'll be a long night if I don't get any sleep." She rubbed her eyes. "It'll be a long night anyway."

The rain was more of a warm mist now. Ken walked down the Money Creek Road, past Maple and the vacant lot, and turned up Main. Nothing was going on downtown—only one of the tellers at the bank was busy, and the café held only Irene Sattle wiping the counter, and some old guy Ken didn't recognize. Through the gap where the alley ran beside the Shangri-la he saw the sodden grass in the Ogema backyard. He thought about Mariah and cursed himself. Max sat on his haunches beside him.

"Well," Ken told him, "we've got to do this sometime."

He walked down the alley, kicking up little wakes in the puddles, the mud squelching around his shoes. Max ran to the Ogema front door and sat there panting, his black coat slick, looking back at Ken.

"I'm coming," Ken called, "I'm coming." He trudged up the walk and knocked on the door.

Jason answered. He was wearing a T-shirt with the Twins logo on it. "You want Mariah?"

Ken turned away from his eyes. Jason knew. Kenny the wonder boy wears a secret outfit almost like Superman's, except it's made of plastic. "If she's in."

Jason nodded and disappeared into the kitchen. Mariah came out of it a half minute later, her arms crossed over her chest, glaring. "What?"

"Can I come in?"

"No. Why are you here?"

"I want to talk to you."

Mariah glanced at Jason as he sat in front of the television. "So talk."

Ken rubbed his neck. She wasn't making this easy. "I think I accused you of something you didn't do."

"Yeah, you did. So?"

"So I want to say I'm sorry."

"So you're sorry. Bye." She started to close the door.

"Jesus, Mariah." He'd come over all this way to humble himself, and she couldn't even be grateful? What's the point of apologizing, anyway? "That's all you have to say? We're friends, aren't we?"

She stopped with the door cracked open. "A friend would never suspect a friend of doing what you accused me of. So how can we be friends?" She started to close the door again.

Ken spoke fast to get his words through before it shut. He was angry enough now to not care what he said. "Could I ever tell you stories about your boyfriend."

She opened the door. "Sam? What about Sam?"

"Sam and Tracy Rux, for one, screwing out at the Hasselquist farm. And then there's the stolen cars he has in the barn. Leo said he saw him out there, making deals."

"Leo?" She laughed. "Since when do you believe Leo?"

"And he kidnapped that bum. The first one, before he was switched."

"You're not still stuck on that, are you?"

Mariah shook her head. "What do you hope to get from this, Ken? You think you can buy my friendship by spreading lies about my boyfriend?"

"I've seen Ricky out there. Sam burns him with cigarettes."

"You're sick, Ken. You need to see a doctor." She shut the door before he could answer.

He stared at the wood, the rain glistening on its surface. Max cocked his head.

"I am seeing a doctor," Ken shouted. "Remember?"

His gaze pounded the wood like a fist, but no one answered it. He stomped away, taking pleasure in the way the puddle water splashed on his pant legs, in his rain-soaked martyrdom. He stopped at the Money Creek Road to let a pickup pass, and his eye caught on the old woodstove. The rain was only a drizzle now, its drops a shiver on the puddles instead of a ripple, but rain is still rain. He thought about the origami and wondered how well that paint can was sealed.

He crossed the street and stepped into the lot, the mud caking on his soles, making him feel a hundred pounds heavier. Water swished in the can when he pulled it out of the oven door. He removed the cover to find the monkeys ruined; the drummer's sticks had decayed into limp spaghetti. He took out what he could salvage—only the old dragon—and put it in his coat pocket.

"Sorry, Ricky," he muttered to the sky.

He didn't yet feel like going home, so he walked by the house to the highway. He stopped at the Get 'n Go while Max waited outside beneath the eaves. Bernette Schmidt was behind the counter, handing change to an old man who shuffled out to an RV almost as big as the store.

"Hey, Bernette."

"Hey, Kenny." Her makeup made her face look like an undercooked steak. "What brings you out on a day like this?"

He shrugged and leaned on the counter. "Just wanted to get out."

"You mountain men just can't stand a day in the house, can you? Got to get out in those hills. You hunt bear out there? You got a gun somewhere?"

"Guns aren't manly enough. I use a sharpened Popsicle stick."

She laughed. "Your brother looked a bit like a mountain man this morning."

"I heard. Did you see him fall?"

"How could I have seen him fall? He drove in dirty."

"He said he slipped coming in for a pop."

Her eyes crinkled, and her makeup flaked. "Then he's telling you stories. He pulled up to a pump and got out of that car of his covered with mud." She laughed. "He's no mountain man. Some of us were made only for asphalt."

Ken studied her and thought about Leo. Nothing was making sense again. He hadn't seized up, had he? Doesn't this medication do anything but make my gums swell and my bowels rumble? "Anyone in the bathroom?"

"That old guy just came out. He was in there forever. I bet it stinks to high heaven."

Ken took the key and went in, and it did. He sat on the toilet, plugging his nose, and thought about Leo, about why he had lied. Maybe all the world, he thought, is the silent place. Maybe sounds aren't really sounds, and what I see isn't really what I see. Maybe I only think people lie; maybe lies are only the way I hear it. Everything gets twisted. Kenny the wonder boy lives in a world of wonder.

But he knew it wasn't true—he couldn't let it be true. Leo had lied. Why had he lied? Why do brothers lie to brothers?

He finished and stood and flushed it all down. He checked his gums in the mirror—Balloon Man—then went out into the store. Bernette was selling a candy bar to a kid who could barely see over the counter.

"See you, Bernette."

"See you, Kenny."

He followed the highway north toward the bluffs, misty gray in the drizzle. He passed the empty Felder house, crossed the bridge spanning the creek, then climbed down onto the far bank, white sand riming his shoes. Max barked and ran on ahead as they entered the trees, chasing squirrel chatter. Ken worked his way up the bluff, his sweat mixing on his skin with the drizzle, until the trees backed away from the clearing where the foundation for the bathwater house stood. He sucked on the sweet forest air, then turned and stared down at the Mississippi River, as gray and still as the highway. He wanted to sit but the stump was wet, so he waited until he'd caught his breath, then followed the trail down to the Forest Road.

Where the trail ended something had burst out of the brush, snapping branches and tearing leaves. The broken branches gleamed white and wet—this had happened recently. Maybe a big buck, he thought. He'd have to tell Sheriff Monson.

But it wasn't hunting season. What reason would a buck have had to run?

Ken searched the ground; Max came back from his trot down the road to help him. There were no clear tracks other than Max's, but the duff had been kicked up. He scanned the road, south toward the Hasselquist bridge and north into the woods. A few feet north, in the muck where the trees met the gravel, he found a footprint. A wrinkled strip ran across it, as if its sole had been taped.

"Ricky," Ken said.

He examined the print more closely. It was fresh—there had been no rain for weeks and the print was too deep to have been made in anything but mud. Ricky had been on the Forest Road since the rain had started that morning. Ken remembered that ride to Winona, remembered stopping for the second Ricky, remembered him tearing the duct tape loose and tossing it onto the highway. This print belonged to the first Ricky. To the real Ricky.

Ken stared back at the broken brush. Why had Ricky come back? What had he been running from?

"Sam," Ken said aloud.

He jogged up the road, his eyes following tracks. Ten feet down he found a second set of big, flat prints following Ricky's. A hundred yards down, the prints mixed as if they'd been dancing and someone had been thrown to the ground. From there they went off again into the woods, the brush not broken this time, the prints more orderly and less widely placed. Sam had chased Ricky down, they'd fought, and Sam had subdued him. He'd taken Ricky into the woods. He must have him tied up again. The basement at the Hasselquist farm leaped screaming into Ken's mind. He imagined lit cigarettes; he could almost smell the stench of burning flesh.

Sam and Tracy were burning Ricky.

Ken studied the trees, the gray sky crying. I can't let it happen, he thought. I can't let it happen again.

Ken stared down at the evidence of the scuffle; he studied the last footprint Ricky had made before it began. It was deep, it was wrinkled; it was smeared at the toe as if Ricky had slipped in midstride. He knelt to examine it more closely; Max almost knocked him over when he came over to sniff it. A white residue had been left behind that must have been caught in the tape.

Ken lifted it with his finger and held it in front
of his eyes. He tasted it and tasted nothing. It
gritted against his teeth.

Ken stared down at his own shoes, at the
sand still clinging to the edges of their soles.
Ricky had run across the banks of Lost
Frenchman Creek, where it emptied into the
river.

"Let's go, Max." He stood and sprinted down
the road.

His chest hurt by the time he reached the
Hasselquist bridge, hurt from fear and excitement and the sandpaper rawness of air being
forced into and out of it. He called Max to his
side and hid in the brush. The barn door was
closed, the trailer home forlorn, the Hasselquist
house staring from its windows as if they were
black and empty eyes. He bolted across the
bridge and down the bank, seeing Sam's big
footprints in the silt there, Tracy's smaller ones.
He sprinted until he reached the cornfield,
leaped into the first two rows, and jogged in a
crouch with his head low, the long leaves knif-
ing wetly across his cheeks. He tripped coming
out, almost went down, then almost tripped
over Max, who ran on ahead, his coat soaked
and shining, his tongue lolling out from the side

of his mouth. To him this was only a game.

They sprinted down the creek with the murmur of the river steadily growing. Ken stopped when he found more footprints, his chest heaving, white flashes lighting up his eyes. Ricky had run along the bank and rock-hopped to the other side. He'd come from somewhere down by the river.

The rain had stopped and the clouds had dropped into a clammy fog, with the mist from the river rising. Ken jogged across the highway into a dream world. Max was a black blur, gray above him, gray around him, white beneath his feet as he reached the sand on the bank near the river. Ken followed more slowly. Thirty yards from the creek mouth he found another set of Ricky's footprints. A long, loping stride, sand kicked back from the toes so hard that it fell in mounds behind the heels, as if he had been dancing over fairy mountains. The other set of prints were five feet closer to the river, just as long and just as loping. He followed them up onto the Felder house's overgrown and weedy lawn, where they faded into soft depressions and occasional smudges. They stopped at the door.

Ken braced his hands on his knees, gasping so hard that he thought he would retch. As his breath calmed, his thinking came back, and he realized he was standing in front of the windows of a house where a kidnapper was holding his victim. Fear leaped into his throat like an animal, and he dived into the bushes beside the steps.

He glanced up at the window above him, seeing nothing but the gray sky reflected. What am I supposed to do? he wondered. He was a scrawny, teenage epileptic with nothing but a pet dog. I could run to the police, he thought; I could call Sheriff Monson. But it would take ten minutes to find a phone, and another fifteen to get hold of him. It would take two hours to convince him that this wasn't a joke.

And meanwhile they were burning him. They were in there right now, and they were burning him. Scrawny epileptic or not, Ken couldn't let that happen.

He wormed his way into the bushes, rose to a crouch, and crawled slowly up the weathered siding until his eyes cleared the windowsill. Inside he saw nothing but an empty room. He dropped again, worked his way around the corner, and checked the window there. Nothing. Farther down along the house he found a small window high in the wall that he guessed opened onto the bathroom. Old drapes, heavy with dust, hung in the first window on the back side of the house. They could have him anywhere in there, Ken thought, and there's no way I can know where. I'll burst in like Dirty Harry with both guns blazing, except I don't have any guns. I'll burst in like Dirty Harry with both fists blazing, and no one will be in the room. When I find the right room Sam's fists will be blazing a hell of a lot hotter than mine and I'll go down, I'll go down. I'll find myself in a chair beside Ricky, smelling the smoke of my burning flesh rising. This is insane.

But they're burning him. His mind wouldn't let that go. They're burning him.

Ken pressed his ear to the window and heard nothing. He checked the rest of the windows and found only empty bedrooms. There was nothing left to do now, he thought, but go in.

He took a deep breath, found the world at the edge of his vision swaying, and sat on the ground with his head down, Max's head crammed into his lap, the dog's big, pleading eyes looking up. Ken felt himself slipping along the tunnel, and he fought the aura down. He rose, checked the back door, and found it locked. The wood of the front door around the knob was scarred as if someone had taken a knife to it, and the knob shone brightly, even in the day's dullness. It was locked too.

He went around to the back again, where he found the remains of a rock garden, littered with mud and weeds. He hefted the largest rock he thought he could toss and stumbled with it back across the lawn. He leaned against the siding, his throat raw and hot, the pit of his stomach deep and freezing.

Max stood beside him, his head cocked to one side, staring at the rock. "Now or never," Ken whispered to him. "Do or die." He crept to a window and checked again that the room was empty. He heaved the rock inside.

He thought the whole world must have heard the glass shatter—some guy in Africa had just sat up from a sound night's sleep and whispered, "What was that?" Ken sprinted across the lawn to the willows along the river's edge, his heart in his ears, his cheeks brush-whipped, his pant legs soaked as he went down in the water. He stared back at the window and waited to see Sam. Max was rolling on his back in the middle of the yard.

"Max," Ken whispered as loudly as he dared, "get your tail over here!" Max rolled onto his belly, stared at him with his tongue peeking out from between his teeth, then rolled over again. Ken could do nothing but pray.

He watched the window through the mist for the space of three heartbeats, for a thousand years. Nobody came to it; not even dull daylight caught on the edges of the broken glass. Ken watched Max and watched the window and still nobody came. Finally, he crawled out of the water and across the yard. Through the broken pane he saw only an empty bedroom, he smelled only air that had been closed up for too long. Maybe Sam was in the basement and hadn't heard the window break. Maybe he'd been too busy to bother.

"Stay here, Max," Ken whispered over his shoulder, but Max was busy hunting crickets in the rock garden and wasn't going anywhere. With his elbow, Ken knocked enough glass away from the sill to crawl through. He jumped up, caught his belly on the ledge, and scooted inside. He fell forward, hitting his forehead on the rock and scratching the back of his hand on a glass shard. He climbed to his feet and waited, rubbing his hand, his heart beating so loudly that he couldn't hear anything else. He felt a warm spot around his crotch, and when he looked down he found he had wet himself.

"I'm a superhero," he whispered. "Kenny the wonder boy steps into a phone booth and comes out Bladder Man." His fear fell into giggles he couldn't control. I must be going crazy, he thought. Nobody in the movies breaks into a house, gets so scared he pisses his pants, then can't stop laughing about it. I'm nuts, I'm bonkers, and it's the funniest thing in the world. He collapsed to the floor in giggles and stared at the closed door. Sam, he knew, would hear him. He waited helplessly.

In a few long, terrible moments he found his fear, and the insanity fell away. He felt as weak as a child.

This room was empty, and that was about all he could be sure of. He cracked open the door and listened, then stuck his head into the hall. He saw nothing. He crept toward the closed door of what he took to be the bathroom—he decided he'd try it first, since he figured if anyone was using it they'd be easier to handle with their pants down around their knees. It was empty. He went down a door, bit his lip, turned the doorknob, and pushed it open—when the hinges squeaked he tasted blood. He clenched shut his eyes and waited for Sam to come bursting out, but Sam didn't. Ken went inside and found the room empty.

He closed the door so he could catch his breath, check the back of his hand and his lip, and grab a scrap of sanity. The hall was still empty when he looked into it. He crept out the door and past a kitchen cluttered with empty cans of pork and beans—a crusted saucepan sat on the stove. He checked another door, choking on his heart, and again found nothing. Every room upstairs was empty. In the front entryway he found a closet filled only with cobwebs. A second door there, he was sure, went down to the basement. He lay on the floor with his cheek against the carpeting, the musty, dusty smell of it filling his nose, and peered beneath the door. A light was on down there.

I can get out of here, he thought. I can leave right now.

But they're burning him.

He crept back to the kitchen and hefted the saucepan. It was too light. He found an unopened can of pork and beans that was heavier and had a good, sharp edge to it. Forget the guns and fists blazing, he thought, I'll hit them with this can—I'll bean them. He broke into helpless, frightening giggles and had to sit on the floor to recover himself. When he was frightened again, when he was thinking as clearly as he thought he was capable of, he crawled across the floor to the basement door. He looked beneath it and sniffed the slight draft blowing through. He smelled nothing.

He rose, found he was hyperventilating, and steadied his breath—epilepsy had proven itself good at least for teaching him how to do that. He turned the knob and pulled the door open, his teeth gritted against the squeak he expected to hear and didn't. He stepped down onto the first step. All was quiet. He stepped onto the second and a part of the basement around the corner opened to him—dusty, empty shelves and a pile of old packing boxes. When he put his weight on the third step, it creaked.

It's now or never, he thought in an instant. They know I'm here and if I don't do something now, it's all over. He roared and charged down the steps with the can of beans cocked beside his ear. He burst around the corner with his scream hoarse in his throat and fear so heavy in his head it made him dizzy. Someone was sitting in a chair beneath a bare lightbulb; a shadow flitted in the corner. He threw the can at the shadow and dived into it and ran his skull into the wall. He collapsed on the floor, his head exploding, and realized the shadow had been his own. He had wet himself again.

Ricky—the *real* Ricky—was tied in the chair in his old jeans and a T-shirt, looking bad, smelling bad, a gag over his mouth. His eyes were big and wild as he stared. Ken rubbed the bump throbbing on his head, then rose when he could and untied the gag. Ricky spit cotton. He looked down at the can, then said, "Jesus, Ken. Pork and beans?"

"It was all I could find."

"Get me loose."

Ken dropped to the floor and frantically worked at the rope holding Ricky's right leg. "You all right?"

"Yeah."

"Your burns all right?"

"What burns?"

He glanced up. "The cigarette burns. Leo told me he'd burned you with cigarettes."

Ricky stared at him. "Leo told you that? Why would he tell you that?"

Ken stopped untying. "He told me that he had you tied up out where he's keeping the stolen cars. He told me he was burning you with cigarettes."

Ricky shook his head. "What stolen cars?"

Ken glanced over his shoulder at the stairway. Any minute, he thought. They'll be back any minute. He worked at the knots again. His fingers stumbled over each other. "You don't know about the stolen cars? Then why did Sam kidnap you?"

"Who's Sam? Nobody named Sam kidnapped me."

One foot was loose, and Ken started on the other. "Then who did?"

"Who else would? Leo!"

The basement spun, and Ken fell backward onto his seat. Ricky sat above him, looking down. Why didn't anything ever make sense? "What do you mean, Leo kidnapped you? Why would Leo kidnap you?"

"Because Leo is Leo. Get my hands loose."

"What's going on?"

"I almost got away this morning. Worked the ropes loose and gave him a shove when he come down and got up the stairs and into the woods, but I got all turned around. He caught me." Ricky nodded at his leg, then glanced at the stairs. "Come on now, untie me before he gets back."

"He's in the Cities. He won't be back for a couple of hours." Ken leaned back on his hands, the floor cold against his palms. His head fell back. He tried to catch his breath, to make sense of the world. "What's going on?"

Ricky shrugged and smiled. "When Leo was on the ship, didn't he ever write you about me? Tricky Ricky?"

"He never wrote me at all."

"I was on the ship with him. If you needed a tool you couldn't find, you came to me. If you needed paint for a bulkhead and the paint locker was empty, you came to me." He smiled again. "And if you needed other things, you came to me for those too."

"What other things?"

"I knew this pimp in Norfolk. We got to be pretty good friends. And it never took me more than an hour onshore in any port to set up arrangements with the locals. And other things? Well . . ." He sat forward as much as the ropes allowed him. "See, me and Leo, we had an arrangement. I could find things, but money to pay for them—it goes right through my fingers. Leo, he provided the financial backing."

"The backing for what?"

Ricky sat back. "Do you know how much a block of hashish costs on the streets of Tangier? Eight bucks. Only eight goddamned dollars! And do you know how much that same block of hashish will sell for in Norfolk or Philly or St. Paul? Let's just say that there's a hell of a markup."

"You were smuggling drugs?"

"One trip," Ricky said, "that's all we did. They brought the dogs onboard when we got back to Norfolk, and that back-stabbing brother of yours planted hash under my mattress while I was up on deck securing lines. Some damned little basset hound sniffed it out. I caught wind and I was gone. I was out of there."

"And they didn't catch you."

"How could they?" He turned his palms up. His smooth forearms reflected the light. "I'm Tricky Ricky." Above his matted beard his eyes narrowed into black slits. "Didn't want to rely on his mother, he said. Said she worked too hard. So he backstabbed me, took my half, and probably sold it for a fortune. I'm getting it back."

Ken just stared. "That first time I saw you, Leo saw you too. That's why all this happened."

Ricky nodded. "I called him up that night to make arrangements. He agreed. We met after you bought me that doughnut. I had the money in my hand, in my goddamned hand, and then I made the mistake of trusting him."

"You should have known better." Ken paused. "I should have too." The ice cream and cow manure were miles apart. Brothers? Hell.

"I turned away. My brain lit up and the lights went out and the next thing I knew I was tied up in a chair in that old farmhouse. You know what crawls around out there at night? Rats. River rats, all slick and shiny."

"Why didn't he just dump you in the river?" Ken knew now what Leo was capable of. "What is he after?"

Ricky smiled again. "There's a difference between me and Leo. See, Leo likes to show off how smart he thinks he is. He bragged to me about all the stuff he was dumping on you, how he paid off some bum who looked a little like me to make an appearance, then get out of town. He bragged how he stole that stereo and set up that scene at the creek—he didn't tell me it was stolen cars, though. Pretty elaborate, when you think about it. Pretty smart. Leo, he's no dummy."

"He's been working on this old car," Ken said. "He's got friends at the junkyards. He must have been out all night buying up junkers after I found the origami."

"He bragged how he had arranged everything to make it look like there'd been a murder, and how when you found me out at the farm he told you that I was being tortured to keep you away. He laughed, God how he laughed. A sucker, he called you. Said he could make you believe anything—all he had to do was play the part of big brother. Said he could have you believing in the Easter Bunny if he wanted."

Something burned inside. "I can almost hear him."

"Me, I know how smart I am. I don't need to show it off. I don't give away what I know."

"What do you know? What do you have on him?"

Ricky just smiled. "I came back only for my half, but after this . . ." He shrugged. "I'll tell you something. I'm sick of this bum stuff. I'm sick of wandering around." He worked his tongue around behind his lip and spit lint. "You know how Leo's always saying, 'Yeah, right?' Now it's my turn. You think you can walk off with my half, Leo? You think I'm going to let you walk off with yours? Yeah, right." He nodded at the rope binding his wrist. "Untie me, so I can get out of here."

Ken closed his eyes. It was all making sense now. Kenny the wonder boy sees the world for what it is. And he sees there's no wonder in it at all.

He stood. He turned his back on Ricky and walked toward the stairs.

"Where are you going? You've got to untie me!"

"To hell with you, Ricky." Ken started up the stairs.

"I'll tell him," Ricky called after him. "You think he'll just let you walk away from this? You'll be sitting here tied up right beside me."

Ken stopped. *"Big?"* Sheriff Monson had asked in the Starlight that morning.

"Not so big," Ken had answered. But with a phone call, Ken would see that Sheriff Monson got his biggest catch of the year. When Leo came back to this basement, he'd find the sheriff sitting in this chair instead of Ricky, and the sheriff would be smiling. Trophy time.

"I swear to God," Ricky shouted, "I'll tell!"

Ken looked back at Ricky. "Where's he going to find a switch for his half brother?" He went up the stairs and out of the house, listening to Ricky's muffled curses and his free foot stomping. Max was waiting at the door.

THIRTEEN

The drizzle outside broke Ken, broke his heart, broke his body, split him open to expose the hot chunk of glowing anger within. He didn't know where he was going—it wasn't until he passed the Get 'n Go that he knew he was even on the highway. Leo, he couldn't stop thinking. Leo.

"I'll be back by seven," Leo had said that morning, *"full of news."*

Ken stared at the sky, at the trees. I'll have news for you too.

When he reached the house he could only think of that phone call. As he walked to the telephone he heard the scratch of bristles on linoleum. Through the bathroom door he saw Therese on her hands and knees beside a bucket, scrubbing the floor.

"You don't have to do that, Mom," he said. "I'll take care of it later."

"I'm almost finished. I've already done the kitchen." She put the brush in the bucket, straightened, and rubbed one arm across her forehead. She left a streak of suds on her brow. "I was too fidgety to sleep."

"You ought to try to sleep, anyway." He reached for the telephone book.

"Who are you calling?"

He wondered what he should say. "Mom, Leo—"

"You're calling Leo?" She smiled from a heavy face crying for sleep. "It's been hard on you both, I know, having a mother who's hardly ever around. But you two have finally been acting like brothers. It makes me proud." She rose to her feet, planted her hands against the small of her back, and stretched. "I've been thinking."

"Thinking what?"

"Isn't there an arts school in Minneapolis? Maybe you should apply. With the way you and Leo have been getting along, you could share an apartment, couldn't you?"

"Mom—"

"Just think of it. One son the head of a business someday, a CEO or whatever they call them. He'll have a membership at a country club somewhere, and he'll have his fancy-schmancy cocktail parties." She smiled. "I've never been to a cocktail party. You suppose he might invite me sometime? I'd probably embarrass him."

Everything inside of Ken was crumbling. "You wouldn't embarrass him, Mom."

"And my other son will be a big-shot artist in New York or Paris or somewhere. You'll have a studio with all that light coming in and canvases stretched with the most beautiful pictures ever painted." She laughed. "I'll bet you'll have those beautiful, naked models running all over too. You artists live a wild life."

He looked at the telephone book in his hand. It was open to Sheriff Monson's number—big and bold against a background of yellow. What was he going to do?

You're not going to do anything, he thought, because whatever you do to Leo you do to your mom. You're not going to do anything.

He closed the book. "El Dorado, Mom."

"What?"

"El Dorado. That's where I'll have my studio."

"Isn't that in California?"

"I'm not sure." All he knew was that it wasn't anywhere he'd been near.

Therese sighed and stretched again. The dreamy look in her eyes faded into dullness. "I think you're right—I ought to try to sleep. But I better finish this floor first." She dropped to her knees and scrubbed again.

Ken watched her for a few minutes, watched the way her arm trembled above the brush, the way her face pulled down, the way her lank, sud-soaked hair hung across her cheeks. She was a thirty-seven-year-old woman going on fifty who'd spent half her life on her knees. You're not going to do anything about Leo, he told himself again. You can't. He set down the book and headed for the door.

"Where are you going?" she called.

"Out."

"What about calling Leo?"

"He'll be home in a couple of hours."

Max was waiting for him in the entryway and stepped back to allow him to open the door. Ken stepped out into the rain—it was falling hard again. He sat on the step and watched the sky, watched the trees, the bluffs wrapped in mist beyond them. Max sat facing him, his head cocked to the side.

"I don't know why I'm sitting out in the rain," Ken told him. "All right?" Max lay on the step with his head on his paws and sighed. He shivered his ears each time a raindrop hit one of them.

Ken pleaded with the sky to reveal to him the wordless question screaming in his mind. I have a half brother and a mother, he told it, and to hurt one means I have to hurt the other. I've got no help from the sheriff, but I've got a broken window and a guy tied up in a basement and my half brother is going to find both in two hours. He'll know the truth then, and I'll be the one left hurting, because Ricky is right—Leo can't let me get away with this. Two hours is all I've got.

I could run, he thought; I could run like Ricky had. But that would wipe the look off of Therese's face and the pride out of her voice. But what Leo was sure to do would do the same.

Run like Ricky had, he thought. I'll grow a beard and bum around the country. I'll ask boys where I can find cheap food, and I'll beg a doughnut from them. Instead of selling origami,

I'll set up a sideshow. Watch Kenny the wonder boy jump into the silent place. It'll only cost you a dollar.

Something was weighing his pocket down, and he stuck his hand in to find it. He pulled out the old paper dragon. The rain dotted its surface, making the paper transparent. Writing seeped through from underneath. His fingers froze and his breath almost stopped.

"Me," Ricky had said, *"I know how smart I am. I don't give away what I know."* But Ricky didn't have much to give away. All he had was his origami.

"The dragon is something special," he had said.

Ken stood and kicked the door open, in so much of a hurry that he left Max out in the rain. He sprinted up the stairs, catching a glimpse of his mother emptying her bucket into the kitchen sink. In his room he shucked off his coat and sat on the bed. He laid the dragon on his lap.

He unfolded the belly and saw Leo's name. He unfolded the head and saw the word *hash*. He unfolded the legs and tail and found himself staring at a sheet of notebook paper with a picture of a ship in one corner. A note had been scrawled across it in Leo's handwriting:

I have duty on the quarterdeck from eight until midnight inspecting bags, so get it tonight. Get two thousand dollars' worth. There's a place up in some pipes we can hide it.

Jesus, Ricky. Two thousand bucks will buy how many blocks of hash? I bet each sells for a hundred back in the States.

Don't screw this up.

Leo

Ken's head was down, his eyes were open, but he could no longer see the note. Instead he saw his half brother on a ship. He saw him plant a block of hashish beneath Ricky's mattress. He saw him laugh about it. He saw Leo in the Felder basement laughing about him.

"A sucker," he had said.

Oh, Leo, Ken thought, you sweet half brother of mine. Who's the sucker now?

It took Ken four tries to refold the
dragon, and even then it looked more like a
dachshund. He slipped his raincoat back on, put
the dragon in his pocket, and hurried into Leo's
room. Leo's stationery was stacked neatly on his
desk.

Ken pulled the stereo out of the drawer and
set it beside the stationery. "Brothers don't lie to
brothers, huh Leo?" he asked as he studied it.

He picked up Leo's pen and saw that his fingers were shaking. He took a deep breath and
held it to steady his hand. In Leo's handwriting,
he began to write.

Just a dragon, Ricky? Yeah, right.

He sat back and studied what he had written and decided it wasn't quite good enough. He pulled a new sheet of stationery off the stack and did it again, but the phone rang and made his hand jump. On his third attempt he was satisfied. He folded the note and slipped it into the same pocket as the dragon.

He changed his pants before he went downstairs. Therese was washing her face in the bathroom sink. She was wearing her Get 'n Go smock.

"What's up?" Ken asked.

She glanced at him over the towel. "Bernette is sick. She called and asked me to come in early."

"You'll miss Leo when he comes home."

"I know, I know." She finished drying her face. "But with the extra money we'll be able to have a real celebration, not one of those one-beer, one-Coke affairs." She glanced at his coat. "You going out again?"

"Not for long."

"Try to have something for your brother to eat when he gets home. He'll be hungry."

"I'll have something for him," he said.

The kitchen clock read 5:30. Max was waiting outside the door, his head down, soaked and glowering. "Sorry," Ken told him. "I have a lot on my mind."

They jogged up the Money Creek Road to the lot. The paint can was lying on its side, the lid cocked open, rain drumming lightly on its surface. Ken picked it up, dried it out with his sleeve, and put the note he had forged inside of it. He tapped down the lid and put the can in the stove, then nodded at Max.

"Let's go."

They jogged past the house and turned north at the highway. Therese's car was parked beside the Get 'n Go. Bernette had just come out of the door and was scowling at the sky—she didn't look any sicker than what a six-pack of beer and a fat boyfriend wouldn't fix. Ken ran by with Max out in front and jogged up the steps of the Felder house. He went down the basement stairs.

"You're a little son of a bitch," Ricky said, "for leaving me tied up down here. What if Leo had come back?"

"He didn't, did he? You want me to let you go?"

"No, I have this thing about chafed wrists and ankles. Of course I want you to let me go."

Time to play stupid. "What do you have on my brother?"

Ricky shrugged. "We're buddies, aren't we, Ken? I mean, you bought me a doughnut and everything, right?"

God, Ken thought, I want to punch him. "Sure."

"Then a buddy would understand that there are some things that can't be talked about."

"You're going to have to promise me something before I let you go."

Ricky studied him through narrow eyes. "Promise you what?"

"Promise me you'll leave my brother alone."

Ricky smiled. "I've decided to do that already. Things get too rough around here."

You liar, Ken thought. You damned liar. He dropped to untie Ricky's leg, keeping his head down so Ricky wouldn't see the rage he felt burning on his face. He worked slowly, not speeding up until he was sure he had himself under control. He pulled the rope free.

"Now the hands," Ricky said.

Ken worked the knots loose. Ricky stood and rubbed his wrists, then headed for the stairs.

"Ricky?"

"Yeah?"

"Don't forget what you promised."

Ricky stopped only long enough to smile.

"You've got my word."

Ken nodded. He had a good idea what that was worth.

Ricky was up the stairs in three bounds and gone. Ken waited until he heard the front door open and shut before he followed him. Ricky did exactly what Ken had expected—he hurried to the vacant lot. He headed straight for the old stove and the paint can within it.

Ken stood in the drive of his house, peeking around the corner of the siding. Max lay under the eaves and out of the rain. Ricky pulled the lid off the can with a grin that froze when he looked inside. He took out the note and dropped the can. As he read it, even from this distance, even with the dirt and the beard and his hair falling over his cheeks, Ken saw his face turn as gray as the sky.

Ricky looked first toward Barney's, then toward the highway. He picked up the can and reached into it again, as if it were a magic hat and the dragon a rabbit. He searched the clearing frantically, then dropped the can and fled toward the highway.

Ken stepped toward the road as he approached. "Where you going, Ricky?"

Ricky jumped and jerked his head. He tripped on the curb and almost sprawled in a puddle.

"Got to move on."

"Remember what you promised."

"I'll remember. That brother of yours, that damned crazy brother . . ." He ran to the highway and turned south, jogging backward, his thumb out. A semitrailer went by in a roar and doused him. Ricky cursed and wiped the mud from his eyes, then turned and ran. Ken watched him until he disappeared.

Max looked up. When he saw Ken grinning, he cocked his head and wagged his tail.

"One down," Ken said.

The clouds in the west were beginning to break—silver spots in the gray. Ken stood at the edge of the highway and reveled in the adrenaline rush that successful revenge can bring. He guessed that it must be six o'clock. He shook off the rush. He only had an hour.

"Come on, Max. We have a lot of work to do."

He went in the house, then jogged up the stairs and kicked open the door to Leo's room. In the back corner of the closet he found Leo's old workboots. Boondockers, they were called in the navy.

"He won't even be able to tell the difference," Ken said aloud.

In a kitchen drawer he found a roll of duct tape. He kicked off his own shoes and put on the boots, then wrapped a foot of tape around the left instep. When he went outside, his feet banged inside the boots as if they were bell clappers.

He thought about sticking to the sidewalk, but was that what Ricky would have done? No, he would have run in and run out, taking the shortest route possible, and that meant trudging through the stretch of dirt beside the walk that the rain had turned to a mud.

What the hell, he thought. It'll leave nice prints.

He ran through the mud, feeling it suck at the boots, feeling the back of his heels rub against the leather. When he reached the road, he turned around and studied his work. Satisfied, he ran back again, going up to the house and kicking open the side door, across the entryway and kitchen, leaving tracks on Therese's clean floor. He took a quick jaunt into the living room—Ricky wouldn't know where Leo slept and would have had to search—then headed up the stairs into Leo's bedroom.

"Time to have some fun," he told Max. Max cocked his head and wagged his tail.

Ken took the stereo and cassette from the desk, then pulled out the drawers and dumped their contents on the floor. He scattered the stationery, turned the desk over, then emptied the closet into the room. He did the same with the dresser. Just to make Leo even more uncomfortable sleeping tonight than he would already be, he stomped mud across the bedsheets. With a pen he pulled the tape out of the cassette, strewing yard after yard of it across the floor. He dropped the stereo on top of it.

He went back down to the kitchen, where he traded the boondockers for his own shoes. He cleaned away the mud and tape in the sink, then went back up to Leo's bedroom and threw the boondockers into the mess.

"It looks just like we had a visitor," he told Max. Max wagged his tail.

The kitchen clock read almost six-thirty. Ken yanked the side door open and jogged outside with Max beside him. They trotted toward the highway.

Ken had one more task to do—he had to make very obvious what was supposed to have happened at the Felder house. He had to make sure it looked as if Ricky had escaped on his own.

At the front step he wiped Max's feet clean, then led him inside—he didn't want a lot of dog prints left in either the house or the yard. He locked the door behind them. They'd leave through the broken window.

All the bedroom doors were open, so he shut them, since they had been shut to begin with and Ricky would not have taken the time to search the house. He climbed down the basement stairs, then kicked at one of the arms of Ricky's chair until he'd broken it. He frayed the rope wrapped around it on its exposed metal brace. It looked good when he finished. He retrieved the dented can of beans and went back upstairs.

He heaved the rock out of the broken window and tossed the beans out after it. He called Max to him and was just about to lift him over the sill when he heard a noise like thunder. The clouds were breaking, the gray almost silver now, and the silver almost blue. Max trotted back into the living room, and as Ken followed he realized that he was listening to a car. Tires ground on asphalt and an engine died. When he looked through the living room window he saw the Buick parked on the highway and Leo jogging toward the front door.

"You think he'll just let you walk away from this?" Ricky had asked.

"Christ," Ken said aloud. "Oh, Christ."

He ran back to the broken window and was halfway over the sill before his panic let him remember that Max was still in the living room. As he sprinted back, he listened to a key turn in a lock, and as he hurried across the living room, one hand holding Max's collar and the other clamped around his muzzle, the shiny new knob on the front door turned.

He dived behind the kitchen counter, holding Max against his body, and slid across the tile until he rammed into the oven broiler's handle. A pain split the point of his shoulder, and his arm went numb. He watched helplessly as his hand fell from Max's muzzle.

"Quiet," he managed to whisper before the front door opened. Keys clinked, and footsteps padded on carpet. Max cocked his head and stared.

"Time for supper, Ricky," Leo called.

He's coming this way, Ken thought. He's coming this way and he'll see me lying here. He's coming this way. . . .

When keys hit the counter, Ken almost screamed. A door opened, then footsteps creaked on stairs. Ken rose to a crouch and ran, dragging Max behind him. He was standing beside the broken window when he found that his arm was too numb to lift Max and heave him outside. Cursing filtered up through the floor, then footsteps pounded on stairs. The front door opened and slammed.

Ken held his breath. He was about to try to heave Max out the window again when he saw Leo sprint around the corner. Ken threw himself down hard beneath the windowsill. Max licked his face, then trotted into the hallway.

Footsteps thudded on grass. Something slapped against wood above him and Ken looked up to see Leo's fingers gripping the sill. Glass dust and flaked paint rained upon his face.

"Oh, shit," Leo said. "Oh, Christ." The fingers disappeared, and footsteps began and faded. Ken called for Max once, twice, and as Max trotted into the room the front door opened and shut. Ken grabbed Max, opened the closet door, and crawled inside. There was no way to shut it from where he was and he had to leave it cracked. He could see the window. He slid into the corner with his hand over Max's muzzle.

The footsteps grew, and Leo ran into the room. He bolted to the window, stared at the glass, and ran his hand over his head. "Oh, god-damn it. Goddamn it!" He turned toward the closet. He was staring at the crack in the door.

Ken's pulse echoed; every time he breathed, his vision flashed. The edge of the world swayed, he felt the terror grip him—a long, dark tunnel spit him out its far end and left him balancing on a fence. Breathe, his mind screamed, breathe, you've got to breathe. But Leo was right there and Ken couldn't breathe, he couldn't think; all he could do was watch and wait and balance on that fence with his arms pinwheeling and pray. He thought he should be praying to God, but he wasn't—God had given him the epilepsy in the first place. He found himself praying to a little pill. He was pleading with a little pill he had taken from the bathroom medicine cabinet that morning and swallowed, pleading with it to take him away from this. It was the only thing that could save him.

Leo's face was twisted into wild rage. He paced from the window to the closet, from the window to the closet, muttering curses, throwing punches at unseen foes. Ken clawed for his breath and prayed.

Leo leaned out of the window, his hands on the sill. Suddenly he stood and pointed. "I see how you did it, you bastard! You did it with a can of beans!"

He laughed wildly, then paced again, his fists clenched, his face livid. "All right, Leo, my man," he said, "you've got to think. Where would he have gone? Back to the lot. Where, if he's not at the lot? To the house maybe, to see if I'd found anything. And if not the house, then he's hitching out of town, probably on the highway." He grinned crazily. "You're thinking now, my man. You're thinking. Damn him. I'll kill him for this." Leo ran out of the room.

Footsteps faded, and the front door opened and closed. The Buick roared and gradually grew softer.

When he'd caught his breath, when the world had quit swaying, Ken weakly pushed the closet door open. Max walked out and sniffed the glass. He cocked his head at Ken.

"It's all right now," Ken told him. He didn't have enough strength to stand. "I think."

FIFTEEN

Ken didn't know what to do. He was afraid to go back to the house, because he didn't know if he'd be able to hide from his face what had just happened. He was afraid not to, because he didn't know what suspicions his absence would raise in Leo. He compromised. He led Max into the living room, then followed him out the front door. They crossed the highway, walked past the Get 'n Go, and hid in the willows and oaks by the river, where Ken could watch the house.

Leo wasn't there. When he came back a half hour later, he parked in the driveway and ran around to the door. A shadow passed by Leo's bedroom window, then Leo ran outside again and studied the muddy tracks running toward the Money Creek Road. He came around the house and paced beside the Buick, his fists clenched, his face wild, shouting at himself. He flung the driver's door open, got inside, and drove to the highway. He turned north.

Ken crossed the yard, went into the house, and sat limply at the table. Revenge is supposed to be sweet and this was, but it had a sour tinge to it. It was revenge wrapped in fear and it was not how he thought it would be. He imagined Leo turning around and racing south on the highway, finding Ricky standing on the shoulder, running him down, then going through his clothing and finding both the note and the truth. He imagined Leo coming back here again. The sourness roiled in Ken's stomach so much that he had to go into the bathroom and crouch by the toilet because he thought he would vomit.

Someone kicked the side door open. Ken could tell by the footsteps who it was.

Through the open bathroom door Ken watched Leo trudge into the living room, collapse on the sofa, and wipe his face with his hands. He looked utterly defeated, and with that look the sourness left and Ken felt very good. Revenge is supposed to be sweet, and this was.

Ken rose and walked into the living room. Leo looked up. "What's with you?" he asked.

Ken shrugged. He felt a mile tall; he felt he could crush his half brother beneath his heel like a bug. "I felt a little sick."

"Dilantin?"

Ken nodded. "How did the visit to the school go?" How did the visit to Ricky go? What kind of a son of a bitch are you?

Leo shrugged. "All right."

"Mom's going to kill you for tracking mud all over the house. She just scrubbed the kitchen floor today."

"What makes you think I did it?"

"Because I didn't." This, Ken thought, feels so good. "Was there someone else in the house?"

Leo's eyes dropped to the floor. His face had the color of overcooked pasta. "All right, I made it. I'll clean it up."

"I'll make you supper while you do."

Leo rose slowly and climbed the stairs to his room. Ken walked into the kitchen, where Max waited by his food dish.

"Hungry?" Ken asked. "I hope Leo is."

Max wagged his tail. Ken opened two cans of dog food.

The pie was just finishing baking when Leo finally came down the stairs. "This place is still a mess," Ken said.

Leo nodded. He had no fight left in him anymore. "I'll take care of it after we eat. What are we having?"

"Your favorite." Ken took the pie out of the oven and set it on the table.

Leo stared numbly at it while it cooled. Ken cut him a piece and slid it onto a plate. The dog food slithered out like leeches. "You having any?" Leo asked.

"Already ate." He handed him a fork.

Leo broke the point off his slice and moved it across his plate. "Remember that Ricky guy?"

Here it comes, Ken thought. He felt like a child on Christmas. "What about him?"

"You haven't seen him around, have you?"

Ken sat. "We took him north to Winona. Don't you remember?" He smiled. "Maybe your memory is funny. Maybe you should be taking my medication."

Leo didn't smile back. He swallowed, then

set down his fork. "I'm not hungry."

"After all the work I did to make this, you have the nerve to . . ."

"I'm not hungry. Let's just leave it at that." Leo stood and climbed the stairs. Ken sat at the table and listened for Leo's bedroom door to open and close. When it did, he set the pie on the floor.

"Two down," he told Max. He thought of Sam—but Sam, as it turned out, had done nothing but cheat on Mariah with Tracy. He thought of Tracy. He couldn't remember ever feeling this powerful before. Max looked up from the pie and cocked his head.

"One to go," Ken said.

SIXTEEN

Leo stayed in his room for an hour.
He had not finished cleaning up the mud before
Ken went to bed. Ken listened to him scrubbing
and felt tickles of joy in his throat. He forced
them down and closed his eyes. He wanted to
get an early start.

Ken awoke before Therese had come home
from the Get 'n Go. He put on his shoes and tied
the laces while Max watched him. He glanced
out the door and thought of Leo, but Leo was
just a bug and not much of a concern anymore.
His mind kept drifting to Tracy. He thought he
had a plan.

"Forgery," he told Max, "is a wonderful
thing."

On his nightstand, beneath his drawing pad, he found the poem that Tracy had given him up on the bluff. He studied her tiny, tight hand-writing—her letters had points like teeth. He felt so powerful, he was giddy.

She made me out to be a fool, he thought, and she enjoyed it. She tore me and Mariah apart. We'll see who the fool is now. We'll see who's torn apart.

It took him a few tries to get her handwrit-ing down. When he finished, he studied his work and smiled.

I've told her, Sam.

The day promised to be as good as the day before had been. He put the note in his pocket, went downstairs, and hurried outside.

The sky was bright. The dew was heavy and cold enough to send shivers through Ken's shoes and up his legs and spine. Max rolled in the grass and came up gleaming. Ken walked down the Money Creek Road, past the lot, and turned onto Main.

The Starlight Café held the usual crowd— Elmer Kelso at the counter with Irene, and Walter Iverson with four complete doughnuts and another half-eaten in front of him. Before

Ken went in he searched the mailboxes beside the door leading up to the apartments—Sam's name had been written in big, blocky letters in what looked like crayon. Ken slipped the note inside it to nestle against a fat, brown sweep- stakes envelope. He went into the café. Max fol- lowed him in and lay by the door.

"Morning, Ken," Irene said.

"Morning."

"Up kind of early."

"A little. Just an orange juice and a dough- nut, please." Ken sat in the back, where the shadows would hide him from the window. "Does Sam O'Hara always come down around this time?"

Mrs. Sattle glanced at the ceiling. "You wait- ing for him?"

"In a way."

"Usually, unless he's been out with that girl- friend." She brought him his breakfast. Ken wondered which girlfriend she meant.

Max sighed heavily and lay by the door with his head on his paws. Ken watched and waited with the light crawling down the wall as the sun climbed higher. The ceiling creaked.

"That would be him," Irene said. "The way he clomps down those stairs, it's a wonder the ceiling plaster doesn't fall off."

Ken waited. The footsteps came down; the door next to the café squeaked open and closed; someone fumbled with one of the mailboxes. The door squeaked again, and the ceiling creaked, louder this time.

Irene glanced up. "Must have forgotten something."

"Must have," Ken said.

As Ken finished the last of his juice, footsteps came down the stairs and the door opened again. Sam did not pass in front of the window.

That makes sense, Ken thought. He's just called Tracy, and he's on his way out to the farm.

Ken gave him a couple of minutes, then stood. He put a dollar on the counter. "Thanks, Irene."

"Say hello to your mother for me," she called after him as he hurried outside.

Sam had just reached the cornfield and was turning west; Ken ran down the alley to Maple, excitement leaping in his chest. He passed by the Ogema house and the cornfield; by the time he could see the bridge, Sam was already pacing in front of it. Ken ducked into the cornfield four rows back and worked his way down, his hand on Max's collar. He stopped when he heard Sam swearing.

Tracy showed up fifteen minutes later. She pulled her bandanna free and tousled her hair. Her shoulders were back, her body defined within her loose clothing. "Hi, Sam."

Sam crumpled the note and threw it at her. It bounced off her chest. "What the hell is this?"

She picked it up and read it. Her eyes flashed up to his, then dropped again. "I didn't write this."

"Don't lie to me."

"I didn't, Sam. I wouldn't."

"Don't lie to me!" Sam's face reddened, and the muscles stood out in his neck. "It must be seven-thirty. How many other people have you lied to today? I'm guessing twenty."

The color drained from her cheeks. She looked like poor little Tracy again. "Sam, I know I've done that before, but I'm not doing it now." Her hand reached timidly for his arm; he knocked it away. "Don't you know how much I care about you?"

"All I know," Sam said, "is that you used me."

"I didn't."

"You use everybody. Well, guess what, Tracy? I'm not some gawky, epileptic kid. I've got a good thing going with Mariah, and you're not going to screw it up."

"But Sam, I'm the one who tells you you'll

make it in Nashville. I'm the one—"

"You," he said. "All you are is some little twit I bang in a farmhouse. You're nothing."

Her head dropped. She collapsed on herself. Was this an act, Ken wondered, or not?

"Don't pull that stuff with me," Sam said. "It only works on fools." He waved his hand over the farmyard. "What we're doing out here is over. Goddamn, I must have been crazy. . . ." His fingers flexed into fists as he scowled at her, then he shook his head and strode down the creek bank toward the river.

"Sam?" Tracy called after him. Her voice was tiny. "Sam?"

Sam didn't answer. Tracy stared at the note, then dropped it. Her face grew hard; her eyes sharper than knives. "You think I need you?" she shouted. "My dad is a doctor in Rochester! I don't need you or anything else in this damned little town!"

Sam didn't answer. The only sounds were the birds in the trees and the creek water gurgling.

"Sam?" she whispered, and then she began to cry.

A breeze kicked up, and corn leaves scratched like claws at Ken's face. What goes around, he thought as he watched her, comes around. He smiled at Max.

"Three down," he mouthed, "and there's only one left standing." He felt his smile spread into a grin—his third helping of revenge was as sweet as the first two had been. Max just stared at him from big, brown eyes.

The bus stop in Lost Frenchman was in front of the bank, and Tracy was waiting there with a suitcase that evening when Ken walked by. He came back and sat beside her. She didn't look at him.

"Leaving?" Ken asked.

"Yeah."

"Where to?"

"Rochester."

The sun was bright on Ken's legs. He studied it; he reveled in the heat gathering there. He couldn't look at her without smiling.

The bus rolled down the Money Creek Road from the highway, whining and spitting exhaust. It pulled to the curb in front of them, its brakes hissing. Ken did Tracy the favor of carrying her suitcase to the luggage trunk. As she handed her ticket to the driver, Ken said, "I know."

She looked at him. "You know what?"

"I know what you told Jack Bjerk."

Her eyes were hard, but she was no tougher than Leo had been the previous evening. She was just another bug.

"Tell me something, Tracy."

"What?"

"Do you have any secrets?"

She didn't answer. She stepped on board with an ugly look on her face. "I don't need any of this, you know," she said. She refused to look out the window as the bus drove away. Ken could do nothing but smile.

Sam didn't show up for work on Saturday morning. When Jack Bjerk checked his apartment, he found it empty.

"He's gone, Jerky," he told Ken that evening in front of the Starlight Café. "And I wanted him to do some more work on my car."

"Why did he leave?" Ken asked.

"All I know is that he had a fight with Mariah. About his singing, I think."

"Where did he go?"

"Who knows?"

Ken just nodded. He hoped there'd be a garage in Nashville that needed a mechanic. It would be the only work Sam would be able to find.

Ken walked down to the Money Creek Road and turned toward the river, Max trotting beside him. A bus went by, and Tracy's face flashed in one of its windows.

"Pretty short trip," Ken told Max.

He was still feeling good enough to take a dig at her again, so he turned around and broke into a jog. Tracy stepped off of the bus and dropped her suitcase and collapsed limply onto the bench. Tears were wet on her cheeks.

"What happened?" Ken asked.

She stood. Her clothes fell loosely. "You wanted to know if I have any secrets?" she asked. "I've got a big one for you." She stepped into the middle of the road and spread her arms. She threw her head back and shouted, "My father doesn't care about me! He doesn't give a damn! And now I'm back in Lost Frenchman!"

Her voice died away, and silence flooded around her. A frightened look covered her face like a mask. She was a little girl hiding in her father's clothing. Just shy little Tracy again.

The good feeling Ken had been enjoying evaporated. No. She was shy little Tracy for the first time.

When she came back for her suitcase, her eyes were down; she was shapeless. "I've got to go."

"Tracy—"

She cut him off with her hand. "No. I've got to go. My mom . . ." Her hand fell limply.

Ken watched her pick up her suitcase and cross the road. She turned south on Maple and was gone, but she had already been gone standing there beside him, folded in on herself until she'd become so small that nothing was left, crumpled like the note Sam had thrown into her chest.

Well, she did it all to herself. But the note, Ken thought. I'd forged it. I did it to her. The revenge soured into bile in his throat.

Max sat on his haunches and watched him. I tried to tell you, his big, brown eyes said, but you didn't listen. You pushed it too far.

Lois Andersen took her prized blue hyacinth to the State Fair during the second week in August and came back with a first-place ribbon. She smiled proudly as she showed it off to Ken.

"Something got into that plant," she said. "I don't know what it was." Max just wagged his tail.

Leo was distracted for the rest of the summer. Twice while working on his car his screwdriver slipped and cut his hand—the second time required stitches that drained the family food budget down to potatoes. He spent his evenings sitting on the trunk of the Buick, his fingers rubbing the bandage on his palm. He fixed his eyes on the highway as if he were hoping someone would come walking down it.

"He's worried about school," Therese told Ken.

"He's worried about something," Ken answered.

Mariah began stopping by the house. She didn't come to see Ken—she wouldn't talk to Ken. She sat on the trunk with Leo.

They went on their first date two weekends before Leo was to leave for school. Ken sat in his room with a sore spot in his chest and watched them drive north toward Winona. He turned away and fell into his drawing, into a gray and white world filled with dark hair shimmering in sunlight.

He came home once from the bluffs to find them kissing in the Buick. He backed away before they saw him, and sat on the front step, staring at the road and the setting sun. This wasn't how it was supposed to be. Ken was the hero of his story, and the hero is supposed to get the girl. But the hero is supposed to make everything come out right, and that isn't how it had

Switch

happened. He'd jumped to conclusions and Mariah hated him. He'd pushed things too far and Tracy had become the pitiful thing he had always thought her to be. So instead of getting the girl, he thought, I'm sitting on the front step and trying not to think about what she and my half brother are doing.

He rose and walked to the corner of the house. They were still kissing. He wanted to tell her the truth about Leo and Ricky, but Therese had been smiling so much lately, bragging about her college boy, and if Ken told Mariah what he knew, then the truth would come back to her and that smile would go away. He hit his forehead with the heel of his hand, then went back to the step.

"I'm so stupid," he muttered.

He threw stones into the road, one by one, each a little harder than the one before it. Max gnawed a bone in the yard, his tail wagging.

-

Leo left for college. Mariah drove up to Minneapolis with him to help him get settled in. He dropped out at the beginning of November.

"I'm failing," he told Ken when he came home. "I can't keep school on my mind."

"Why?"

He shrugged. "I worry about things."

Therese's face was ashen when Leo told her. "What do you mean, you're quitting?"

"I played the game long enough to see how it works, Mom," Leo explained. "School isn't teaching me anything the navy can't."

"So you're going back into the military?"

Leo shrugged. "Seems wise."

Therese ran her hand back through her gray-flecked hair, then over his. Her face was heavy and long and she sighed. "You do whatever you want to do."

"I don't want to disappoint you."

"You're not disappointing me." She smiled. "You do the right thing and you can only make me proud."

Leo had to go to naval reorientation at the same place he'd gone for boot camp, just north of Chicago. He came home for leave before being transferred to Norfolk, to the same ship he'd been stationed on during his first enlistment. On the day Leo left, Ken watched him say good-bye to Mariah from his bedroom window—Leo kissed her, and she cried. Ken watched her cross the road and head toward Maple, her shoulders slumped, her head down—she looked a lot like Tracy. He went down to the car. Leo was stuffing his duffel bag into the trunk. His boondockers were laced through its handle.

"Everything all right?" Ken asked. "I mean between you and Mariah."

Leo's eyes followed her down the road. "She'll be all right. I'm having her come out to Virginia after she graduates."

"Everything all right with you?"

"With me?" Leo shrugged. "Why wouldn't it be?"

Ken shrugged too. A bug, he thought. Leo, you are a bug I don't dare crush. "I've got a going-away present for you." He reached into his pocket and fished out the old dragon.

Leo took it and ran his fingers over its creases. "I remember this. That bum made it, didn't he? Not the second one—the one before Sam switched them. What was his name?"

"Ricky."

"Why you giving this to me?"

Because it's the truth, Ken thought. What are you going to do with it? "No reason."

Leo studied it, pursed his lips, then nodded. "I'd have to carry it in my duffel, and it would get crushed." He handed it back. "And to tell you the truth, I've got no use for it."

Ken nodded as he put it back in his pocket.

He held out his hand and was almost surprised when Leo took it. Ice cream and cow manure meet again. "Have a good trip."

Leo nodded. "Sure." He shut the trunk and went back into the house.

Therese was with him when he came out again, her arm around his waist and tears heavy in her eyes. Ken waited as Leo kissed her and got into the car, then stood beside her as the Buick bottomed out while backing onto the road. Leo turned onto the highway and headed south, in the same direction Ricky had gone.

Therese put her arm around Ken's shoulder. Her lower lip trembled. Ken knew it was worth not telling her. It was worth everything in the world.

"Aren't you working tonight?" he asked.

"Yes." She wiped her eyes with both hands, then smiled. "That damned Bernette. She wants me to come in early again."

"A boyfriend?" Ken asked.

"Some big slob from over by Money Creek." She yawned. "Just thinking about him makes me tired. I think I'll get some sleep."

Ken followed her to the side door. She kicked it open, and Max slithered in in front of them. Therese went up to her bedroom; Ken followed her up to his. Max jumped up on the bed, and Ken lay on his haunches.

Ken took the dragon from his pocket and ran his fingers over its creases, just as Leo had done. He set it on the nightstand and picked up his drawing pad.

He rubbed his finger across his swollen, painful gums. He was Balloon Man. He was Kenny the wonder boy. He lived in a world of wonder.

"Things get kind of funny," he said to Max.

Max cocked his head. His tail thumped twice on the mattress before he lay back and sighed.

A few seconds later, Ken was lost in a gray and white world.